"You don't have to be a Chargers fan to relate to Ross Warner. If your team has ever hurt you or let you down, you already get it. Sadly, that's all Ross and I know. I have known Ross for 4 decades and we have shared our football frustrations and dashed hopes more times than I can remember, (but Ross recalls every one.) We are all Ross Warner and *Drunk On Sunday* is his therapy. It's up to us to let him know that we understand. That being said, the Chargers better win a Super Bowl during our time on Earth or I'm gonna be pissed."

> **—Eric Stangel, Emmy-winning Writer/EP *The Late Show with David Letterman*, Chargers fan since 1979, and friend of Ross' for life**

"Ross Warner cuts through the haze of stoned Saturdays and drunken Sundays with sharp and direct prose that illuminates the struggle to become a man while retaining boyish enthusiasm for life. It perfectly encapsulates the fight to balance love of family with love of football and music, constantly buoyed by a soundtrack as essential to this story as it is to life's everyday experiences. He brings to life a story that many of us can intimately relate to."

> **—Alan Paul, *New York Times* Bestselling Author, *One Way Out: The Inside Story of the Allman Brothers Band* and *Texas Flood: The Inside Story of Stevie Ray Vaughan***

"It was the week prior to Christmas, 2004 and the San Diego Chargers were in Cleveland to clinch their first AFC West title in a decade. There was bitter cold and heavy snow. I had to return immediately to New York, but there was a serious concern possibility that all flights would be cancelled. As I sat at the gate, I met a devoted Charger fan, Ross Warner, who had flown in for the game. Since we had won the game, he wasn't the slightest bit concerned about getting home. Our conversation turned into a long relationship in which I learned about his total dedication to the Bolts. I saw him at numerous games throughout the years. He has seen the team everywhere. His fandom and his knowledge are unparalleled. Clearly, he loves his Chargers."

—Jim Steeg, Former Executive Vice President and Chief Operating Officer, San Diego Chargers

"In nearly three decades of covering the Chargers, I've come across few fans as passionate and as witty as Ross Warner. He has countless tales and he knows how to tell them! I'm looking forward to his book, *Drunk On Sunday.*"

—Jay Paris, Former Chargers Beat Writer and Author of *Game Of My Life: San Diego Chargers*

"Even as a Bills fan, scarred for life by Dan Fouts to Ron Smith with 2:08 left, I *still* enjoyed this tale. It's terrific, and right up there with Frederick Exley's *A Fan's Notes.*"

—Rich Blake, *Talking Proud: Rediscovering the Magical 1980 Season of the Buffalo Bills*

DRUNK ON SUNDAY

DRUNK ON SUNDAY

. . . .

ROSS WARNER

NFB

BUFFALO, NEW YORK

Published by NFB, Buffalo New York.

NFB is an imprint of No Frills Buffalo/Amelia Press
119 Dorchester Road
Buffalo, NY 14213

For more information visit
nofrillsbuffalo.com

Cover design by Kyle Bateman.

Interior design and layout by Mulberry Tree Press, Inc.

trade paperback ISBN: 978-1-7338764-8-3

Drunk on Sunday is a work of fiction. Characters, organizations,
events, and places (even those that are actual) are either products of
the author's imagination or are used fictitiously.

To my parents, Donald and Linda,
who both left this earth just a little too soon,
but who sacrificed everything in order to teach
me how to live. Of course, I'd have no stories
worth telling if not for Sam. You not only gave
me a reason to grow up, but helped create
Aaron and Sarah to make sure I stay that way.

Love, Ross

"I'd probably listen more
if you talked a little less."

—Samantha E. Warner

CONTENTS

PART I: FOLLOW THE DREAM YOU SEE ONSCREEN • 15

Strangest of Places • *17*

Suburban Incubation • *18*

My Kind of Zoo • *22*

Lightning-Fueled Lunacy • *25*

Get on the Bus • *28*

An Obsession That's Pleasin'? • *33*

Shakedown on Seventh Avenue • *39*

Adrift but Not Alone • *44*

Live More, Think Less • *47*

One More Saturday Night • *52*

Just Ride • *56*

Don't Worry About the Destination • *60*

March Winds Blow Through Nassau • *65*

The Proper Potion • *68*

Time to See with Both Eyes • *76*

Kinda Frightening • *84*

Sunday Morning, Whip Coming Down • *88*

Wander 'Round • *92*

Can't Take It with You • *99*

PART II: BETTER TO SEARCH SINCE YOU CAN'T STAND STILL • 105

Sing for Your Subway Fare • 107

Full of the Blues • 110

Following the Dream • 114

Drunk on Super Sunday • 120

Almost Ablaze at the Creek • 126

The Broken Angel Sings No More • 135

Dial "0" for Jobless • 140

Ebony & Irony • 143

Lightning Bolt of Inspiration • 147

Write About That • 150

I Call Myself the Teacher? • 155

I Knew Right Away • 159

Take Root in the Earth, But Keep a Place in the Stars • 163

Fuck the Fear • 169

Not Sure I Want This • 173

Join the Club? • 179

Makes the Dream Come True • 184

Words While Wasted • 187

A Promise Worth Making, Finally • 194

Jump a Little Higher as We Reach the Morning Light • 198

Growin' Up? • 205

Living in Doubt • 209

The Prize I See in Those Eyes • 212

Acknowledgments • 219

About the Author • 220

DRUNK ON SUNDAY

PART I:

Follow the Dream
You See Onscreen

Strangest of Places

"MR. GROSS, WOULD LIKE to *hold* your daughter?"

Sarah hadn't even opened her eyes yet. Her lids looked like they'd been welded shut. She had a dusting of reddish hair and had now been in the world for an entire minute without making a sound. Was something wrong? When she finally opened her mouth, it extended so wide that I thought she was yawning for a second. As I was about to fully spiral with anxiety, I was brought back by the most unearthly sound.

"WAAAAAAAAAAGGGGGGGGGGHHHHHHHHH!"

I craned my head over the partition. Sammy, who'd just endured the cesarean section to bring our daughter into this world, looked up with those beautifully mismatched eyes (one hazel and the other brown). All the tension in my body seemed to escape through some secret valve. She could always do that for me when I needed it most. Sarah opened her own beautiful eyes to reveal two hazel pools. Maybe she'd inherit some of Sammy's calming magic. Neither of us had Sarah's red hair, although I did have dark orange as a baby before it turned brown. People would eventually ask if she was the milkman's, which was both outdated and downright disrespectful if you really thought about it. I spent my whole life searching for a girl with whom to enter adulthood (while simultaneously running from her). God knows she'd have had her reasons for leaving more than once along the way.

I couldn't yet tell if Sarah resembled either of us. Her face was as smooth as a statue's, with only a few defined features. I knew that lines and creases would appear as she grew and experienced things. She had only been alive for a few minutes, but I already knew how much I wanted to keep her safe. I knew I'd also have to let her make her own mistakes. I just hoped I didn't turn into one of those clichéd new dads from the movies.

By "movies," I meant the type I avoided seeing. The films, music, and books I liked never showed guys turning into parents. They were all about becoming free and staying that way. Then again, maybe I (and the guys who created them) weren't all that free to begin with.

Suburban Incubation

BEFORE BECOMING the home of Bill and Hillary Clinton, Chappaqua was just a wealthy Westchester hamlet about forty minutes north of New York City. Like many other suburbs, there always seemed to be an air of phoniness around it. For instance, some roads remained unpaved thanks to the vigilant desire of its residents to preserve the town's "bucolic setting." However, those same residents drove their Porsches down those streets.

Like so many of my generation, living in the suburbs probably caused me to rebel against entirely fabricated (or at the very least exaggerated) forces. It's not as if I was oppressed at home. My parents were actually quite loving and extremely tolerant of my often ill-fated attempts to be an outsider in the most cookie-cutter place on earth. Their support was even more necessary since my sister Liz, three years younger than I was, was a perfect child by comparison.

My parents were lifetime New Yorkers who met in the early 1960s at the University of Rochester. My mom was from upstate Rome, famous for its proximity to Griffiss Air Force Base and the site of "Woodstock '99," the ill-fated attempt to reboot the original festival at an alternate location. Of course, that concert will be forever associated with Limp Bizkit, fires, and numerous tales of sexual assault. On a more positive note, my mom was the second person to become a bat mitzvah in that town after her parents moved from Austria at the beginning of World War II. Upstate New York must have seemed like paradise for Jews after Vienna.

My dad hailed from Mount Kisco, adjacent to Chappaqua, but working-class by comparison. That wasn't saying much, but the town was stocked with tough Italian kids that I naively imagined as rejects from *West Side Story.* My dad told me that they picked on the Jewish kids simply because they felt that they could. That pissed me off until he also told me that my grandfather got a chance later to exact some revenge through his role as the town's District Attorney. I hated the idea of anti-Semitism, but was attracted to the idea that being Jewish made you a little different. If being an outsider was a problem for anybody else, that was on them. Plus, you might get a little karmic comeuppance along the way. If you were really lucky, you might be the one to dish it out.

As I later saw myself as some sort of a sarcastic antihero, this was to be my origin story. My mom got her first taste of my outlaw behavior when she received the following phone call when I was in nursery school:

"Mrs. Gross, this is the Chappaqua School for Childhood Transitions. We regret to inform you that Robert had a rather difficult day."

"Oh? What did he do?"

"Well, he ran off during recess and proceeded to pull his pants down and defecate in front of the other children. I'm assuming he is not yet potty trained?"

"Sadly, he actually is."

"Well then why would he do such a thing?"

"I will certainly ask when I come to get him."

While this was the end of my public pooping habit, the overwhelming question as to why I did these things would remain a mystery to me for many years. I'm still not sure I've got it all figured out, but at least this incident could be partially blamed on my consumption of about half a pound of Play-Doh. There also may have been a crayon or two in there. That's a lot of roughage for a little kid.

But this was only the first in a pattern of outbursts my parents endured. Next up was my first day of kindergarten. It was the fall of 1976 and I had a giant dome of brown hair with a few swirls and waves that defied the laws of physics. My look was conventional for the period so I think I tried to compensate by bucking the system. "The system" in this case happened to be one of the best school districts in the country, rather than some authoritarian regime, but I didn't know that yet.

Our teacher seemed very pleasant and had one of those dresses with pockets in the front. She had both hands inside of them as she addressed the class:

"Okay, boys and girls," she said. "We're going to start with a little game. This will also let me get to know a little bit about you."

This wasn't so bad. At least she was starting class with a game.

"I have put a letter in front of each of you. You are going to use this letter in a complete sentence. While sitting Indian-style, 'criss-cross apple sauce,' turn over your card and read your letter to yourself."

It was a good thing that she told us that last part because when I spotted the letter *I*, I almost erupted. What word could I possibly come up with, let alone a *sentence*? Before I could even deal with my resulting frustration, the girl to the teacher's right started things off.

"*K* is for kangaroo!"

We all had nametags, so the teacher was able to instantly give personalized feedback.

"That's great work, Amy! Now let's see what the rest of the class comes up with."

I looked at the twelve kids in the circle that stood between me and Amy. I needed to come up with something quick. I knew the boy to the right since we had been in nursery school together. Dawson looked at his tile and saw the letter *J*.

"*J* is for jump," he whispered.

While that was nice to know, that tidbit didn't give me any bright ideas. I racked my six-year-old brain for any word I could use. I was so preoccupied that I didn't even notice when all the kids before me had taken their turn. I looked down at the over-sized *I* for one last possible bolt of inspiration.

Nothing.

"I is for icky, like our teacher."

It felt completely natural and spontaneous, even though it was neither.

"Rob! That's not very nice. Why would you say such a thing?"

As I served my subsequent time out, I thought about what caused me to insult a woman I had only known for thirty minutes. It was frustrating and a little demeaning to have to watch the other kids playing with blocks. I considered pointing this out, but this was half-day kindergarten and we also got about ten play breaks a class.

This well-intentioned educator certainly didn't deserve my wrath. She was simply the first authority figure I met outside my house and I responded accordingly. I projected my frustration on her, but in my defense, she could have given me a much better letter to work with.

My Kind of Zoo

"LET IT GO." Before these words dug earworms into millions of kids' minds via *Frozen,* they were the ones most uttered by my parents during my childhood. When my mind got ahold of something, it usually got stuck there. If my mom took me to buy sneakers, I'd end up repeatedly trying on different sizes to make absolutely sure they fit.

"They're going to be on *your* feet," she'd remind me.

She was trying to calm my fears, but it had the opposite effect. Even if the shoes felt completely comfortable, I'd often wear them inside until I felt ready to tackle the anxiety that came with risking the elements. It wasn't until 10th grade that I was unsurprisingly diagnosed with obsessive compulsive disorder, and even then it was the days before medication was used in such cases. I was (and am) far more obsessive than compulsive and tried to think of the anxiety as just another thing at made me a little different. I started seeking other outsiders I could identify with.

Television didn't offer that yet, so I looked to the movies. My mom took me to the ones I wanted to see since I was too young to go on my own. I saw *Star Wars* and *Grease* during their first runs in theaters this way, but the movie I wanted to see most of all was *Animal House.* I remember when I first saw the "one-sheet" ad in my parents' Sunday *New York Times.* The animated poster looked like one of my *MAD* Magazines, only much better. It had horses, motorcycles, cheerleaders, and guitars. I didn't know what the movie was about, let alone what these things had to do with it. I just knew I had to see it.

There was a short-lived TV series called *Delta House* which my parents let me to watch. John Belushi wisely refused to be in it, so ABC had to create his brother, "Blotto," played by Zero Mostel's son looking like an off-brand Josh Gad. The show aired on Saturday nights, the "family hour" back then. Of course, it was awful, but if the sanitized version was *that* bad, then the real deal must have been *that good*. VCRs and cable television were a couple of years away (at least for me), so it didn't seem like I'd have much of a chance to find out for myself.

But the following fall, another cartoon-like ad in the newspaper gave me renewed hope. The top of the page simply said "GUESS WHO'S BACK?" I immediately knew what was coming next.

All of the Deltas had their backs turned to a bunch of pissed off characters from that first poster, including a dog, a miniature devil, and a guy holding *his own fucking head upside down*. Only one face looked back from the Delta side, the real Bluto. "The Most Popular Movie Comedy of All Time," it read. It was as if John Belushi himself was making sure I didn't miss my last chance to get in on the fun.

I begged my parents to let this be my first R-rated movie, but I wasn't even thinking about the inevitable raunchiness. The Deltas looked like the ultimate outlaws, yet somehow seemed to be the heroes of the story. My parents eventually relented, but gave my grandfather the job of accompanying me. They probably thought they'd be less responsible for my subsequent corruption that way.

On the surface, he was an unorthodox choice for the job. My grandfather's experiences in Vienna before emigrating had left him a very hardened man. My mom told me that as tough as he was as a dad, he seemed happiest being my grandfather. The day he took me to *Animal House,* he definitely seemed happy. I spotted a big smile break out on his face the first time naked breasts appeared on the screen. Of course, I was only looking in his direction to make sure he wasn't going to make us leave. Once that keg crashed through the window to the strains of "Louie, Louie," I knew I couldn't take that.

Seeing the movie for the first time affected me the way other people talk about *Star Wars. Animal House* formed the basis of everything I thought was funny from that moment forward, but had an even deeper effect. The Deltas didn't fit in anywhere but with each other. They were misfits who were free to do as they pleased. I recognize that there are plenty of aspects of the movie that haven't "aged" well, but the movie was my first introduction to the freedom of being an outlaw. As a brotherhood of outsiders, the Deltas had infinitely more fun than they would as individuals. Plus, the Omegas and the school administration were the real villains with the way they treated their pledges, girlfriends, and wives.

I didn't really identify with the boorish behavior represented by John Belushi's "Bluto," anyway. I was more like Boon, the Jewish wise-ass. He also got the girl that I'd eventually know from *Raiders of the Lost Ark*. Boon's inability to grow up and adjust to life outside the fraternity might have lost him that girl more than once in the movie, but I didn't pick up on that lesson. I only saw the amazing possibilities presented when you pushed things to the edge. I'd find out eventually how easy it was to go off the cliff.

My grandmother was also an influential presence in my life. When she came to the United States after being fortunate enough to escape Austria, she always tried to help others. She gave back by raising tons of money for Hadassah, the women's Jewish service organization. I'm also sure that wasn't popular with all the residents of Rome in the 1950s. But as proud as she was as a Jew, her family always came first. There was nothing she wouldn't do for the people she loved. When she and my grandfather eventually moved down to Florida, she was on the board of their development. My sister and I spent many vacations during elementary school at their condominium in Surfside, the most Jewish section of Miami. When the other residents complained that I had peed through my diaper into the pool, she came to my defense instantly.

"You think all of you 'alta kockers' haven't pished in the pool at least once?"

She also took my sister and me to Disney World all by herself, even though it was clearly too much of a strain. She'd even watch us from time to time when our parents went away without us. They knew she was far more lenient than any of our babysitters, so my parents made me promise that I'd check in with her any time I left the house. When one of my friend's moms asked me to stay for dinner after a day of playing basketball, I called home. My grandmother picked up the phone on the first ring.

"Grandma, it's Rob. Listen, Mom and Dad said that—"

"Rob? I'll see if he's here."

Before I could respond, she put the receiver down and walked off. I could hear her calling my name and I hoped she'd at least find my sister to explain. But after a couple of minutes, she got back on the phone in a heightened state of confusion.

"Hello? Rob's not here. I'm sorry."

"No, Grandma, you don't understand. This *is* Rob." But before I could get any further, she cut me off again.

"Oh, Rob! You have a phone call." And with that, she hung up on me.

At least my parents were able to enjoy most of their weekend before my grandmother mistakenly informed them I was missing.

Sometimes a story is too good to be made up.

LIGHTNING-FUELED LUNACY

"I WILL ALWAYS be a Chargers fan."

I still remember making that silent pledge to myself at the bus stop, which was actually my parents' driveway. I said it to myself so seriously that I knew it wasn't bullshit. It was like Bruce Wayne's stated crusade to avenge his parents by protecting Gotham City. Kids make promises like that all the time about sports teams.

They wear the hat or jersey of whatever team or player is in vogue that season and move on once the losing starts. But I wasn't built that way, as I would find out time and time again. There were days, weeks, and even entire seasons, where I regretted that pledge at the bus stop. Yet at the time, it didn't even feel like a decision.

I first took notice of the Chargers after they destroyed the Steelers in the middle of Pittsburgh's second batch of back-to-back Super Bowl championships, by the score of 35-7 on Monday Night Football. But it was how the Chargers scored those 35 points that got my attention. Dan Fouts, their quarterback, didn't look like any football player I had ever seen. He had a bushy beard that spilled out from beneath his chinstrap and his Bunyanesque appearance seemed even more exaggerated since he ripped all his jerseys at the collar. It was as if the regular conventions of pro football couldn't contain him. He even moved differently than other quarterbacks. After receiving the snap, he backpedaled rather than turning to his side to drop back for the pass. The contrast of his hulking frame retreating with a dancer's gait made it seem like he was almost tiptoeing away from the defense.

But once he was in the pocket and safely behind his blockers, he became anything but delicate. Fouts always looked like he was throwing a deep pass even when he wasn't. From the way he heaved it, the ball looked like it weighed fifty pounds. His resulting passes were often wobbly but deadly accurate. The "Bolts," led by their innovative head coach Don Coryell, seemingly threw on every down. Anyone could be Fouts's intended receiver each time he dropped back. His goal was to get the ball into the end zone as quickly as possible. With "Air Coryell," touchdown bombs were frequent and acrobatic catches became routine. Like the Deltas, they looked like they were having the most fun in their own way. I didn't know at the time that during each week of practice, Fouts wore a hat that said "MFIC." It stood for *Motherfucker in Charge*. You can't get any more outlaw or any cooler than that. The Chargers played the style of football

I wanted to mimic on the playground. The "smashmouth" style of the Steelers and Cowboys required run blockers, anyway. What grade school kid wanted to protect the quarterback at recess?

After that pledge at the bus stop, I quickly learned why they call it being a "die-hard" fan. In '79 the Chargers were upset in the first round of the playoffs when the underdog Houston Oilers deciphered their offensive signals. The following year, they beat the Bills when Fouts found rarely-used receiver Ron Smith with 2:08 to go. However, they lost the next week to the archrival Raiders on their own field and fell a game short of the Super Bowl. The next year they blew a 24-0 lead to the Dolphins in their first playoff game, but survived in overtime. The "Epic in Miami" is still widely considered the greatest football game of all time for all of its dramatic twists and turns. It was certainly the most exciting, though all I felt while watching was that the Chargers were going to choke their giant lead away.

Their reward for outlasting the Dolphins in 88-degree weather was to travel to Cincinnati and face the Bengals in -9 degrees below zero cold. With the wind chill, it was the coldest day in NFL history, at -37 degrees below. By kickoff of the "The Freezer Bowl," Dan Fouts had actual icicles on his beard. He couldn't even feel the ball, let alone throw it. He still claims to this day to experience frostbite symptoms and the Bolts lost by 20. They were one game short of the Super Bowl for the second straight year, while appearing in two playoff games so legendary they earned their own nicknames.

The loss at Cincy was tough to take, but within a couple of years, the Chargers weren't even making the playoffs. Don Coryell was fired in 1986 and Fouts announced his retirement the following year. Before I knew it, the team was consistently finishing in last place. Yet the worse they got, the stronger my resolve to support them became. This dedication would become an integral part of my personality. My obsession with the Chargers took me to a ton of strange places, both literally and figuratively. The only thing I can compare it to was the first time I saw another bearded non-conformist perform for the first time. But my first Grateful Dead concert was still eight years away at this point.

GET ON THE BUS

THE THINGS I WAS DISCOVERING felt like more than simple interests, as they would eventually become lifelong obsessions. They felt like secrets shared only with me.

I started wearing the same outfit to high school every day, an unbuttoned flannel with a short sleeve shirt showing underneath. Most of them were either Chargers T-shirts or souvenirs from some family vacation. Nowadays, they would be sold at Urban Outfitters, but being "distressed" is not the same as being authentic. I found this out the when I bought a shirt at the mall with The Police printed on it during my sophomore year of high school. I was so excited to show it off until I walked past the school's outdoor smoking section while wearing it.

I usually steered clear of that part of school, but was feeling so good that I lost focus. All it took was one word to snap me out of it.

"HEY!"

I turned around and found myself looking into the eyes of the closest thing Chappaqua had to a dirtbag. It had been a week filled with beautiful spring sunshine, yet somehow his pasty face hadn't absorbed a single ray. Then again, it was hard to see anything under that wondrous mullet due to the sea of red pimples. As scared as I was, I couldn't help but walk towards him. He was too scary to ignore outright. I got right up to the edge of the paved walkway without setting foot on the dirty macadam.

"You like The Police?"

"Well, yeah," I mumbled.

"Did you catch their show in June?"

"I, uh . . . no."

"So basically you're wearing a shirt from a show you didn't even go to. Where'd you get it, at the fuckin' *mall*?"

Before I could respond, he started back in. "Listen, I'm sure you didn't know any better, but you don't wear the shirt if you didn't see the fuckin' band in concert. That's almost as bad as wearing the band's shirt *to* the show." Years later, I'd hear that second piece of advice in 1994's *PCU* (a highly underrated movie, by the way). At the time, however, these rules were completely unknown by me. This kid was teaching me how to avoid being a poser, though I'm sure he just wanted to give me shit.

As he turned around to walk away, I spotted the portrait of Jim Morrison painted on the back of his denim jacket. I was about to mention that there was no way for him to have actually seen The Doors before I thought better of it. There would be plenty of times where I wouldn't be as cautious. My sarcasm may very well have been a coping mechanism, but I began using it like a weapon. This brought varied consequences in the very near future.

It was before I had my driver's license and I still rode the bus. I was about to catch it home one afternoon when I noticed a white Ford Mustang kicking up a ton of dust in the dirt lot next to the actual parking lot. A bunch of kids watched someone do donuts while "Summer Nights" from the Sammy Hagar-led Van Halen blared from a boombox. It was as pathetic as it sounded. I turned to my friend Dawson and muttered that being on the bus suddenly didn't seem so lame.

What really got to me was how in awe the rest of the kids were of this display. I couldn't even drive, but I was pretty sure that going in circles didn't warrant such an audience.

"Dawson, I think the Guidos need a new soundtrack."

I didn't even realize how loud I said it until all those goofy grins straightened out, seemingly in an instant. This was the '80s, and no one attributed any racial overtones to that term. But you didn't call out a group by their own name, as I was about to find out.

"Gross! What did you fucking say?"

I turned to get on the bus when I realized that there was a line ten people deep in front of me. All I caught was a glimpse of black hair before hitting the ground. Through the one ear that wasn't stuck in the dirt, I heard the taunts of my attacker.

"You think you're pretty funny. Too bad you aren't as good at fighting."

"Actually I can really put the Jew in jujitsu," I mumbled back.

The circle of kids around us, seemingly bigger by the second, all laughed. I was impressed at how quickly I found a comeback, especially one that good. But the fact that my new adversaries didn't get or appreciate my humor just seemed to make them angrier. I decided to double down regardless.

"Didn't you know, I'm a regular Bruce Lee-bowitz."

Judging by the crowd's laughter, I had picked the perfect response. But as Chappaqua's finest gearheads rumbled towards me, I knew I wouldn't have time to soak in the adulation. For all I knew, these could have been the sons of the guys who tortured my dad's high school classmates. Dawson grabbed me after they got a few punches and kicks in. By the time I was back on my feet, two assistant principals had them corralled. Fortunately, I never received any discipline for my inflammatory comments. More importantly, those guys never sought any retribution from me. Getting my ass kicked must have given me a little parking lot adjacent credibility.

Without a car, though, I couldn't get to any of the house parties my classmates threw while their parents were out of town. I hadn't yet been invited, but that was beside the point. I was waiting for my bus a few months after my near-stomping when a silver Volkswagen Scirocco pulled up to the curb. Jeff Green-berg, who had never spoken to me before, leaned out of the window to ask if I wanted a lift home. His cartoonish grin explained why everybody called him Barney Rubble.

When I got in the back of the car, I immediately noticed that there was already another kid in the passenger seat. "Greeny," as everybody called him to his face, told me I could climb in the back.

"This is Tap. Tap, this is Rob Gross, the guy who kind of got the shit kicked out of himself over there in the parking lot."

Tap, whose brown hair almost completely covered his eyes, seemed interested.

"How did that go?"

"Actually, it was *next to* the parking lot."

"He fucking told off the Guidos," Greeny interrupted. "They were blasting that Van Hagar shit! Dude, you're like that guy in *Animal House* who got beat up in the hotel room when Neidermeyer called him an asshole."

He was combining the storylines of Pinto and Boon, but the reference alone was welcoming. Being in a group, if only for a few minutes, made me feel better than I thought it would. I recognized Led Zeppelin blasting through the car's speakers.

"'Your Time Is Gonna Come,'" said Tap. "It's off their first record. That shit's just pure rock before they got all acoustic a couple albums later. Don't even get me started on "Stairway" and the rest of *Zeppelin IV*. The smoking section kids all have that guy in the cloak painted on their jackets like they're getting ready for a Dungeons and Dragons game."

I only knew this kid as Greg. I asked how he got the name Tap.

"It's 'cause of this." He pulled out a black pump, with a long tube attached to one end and a silver needle to the other. "It's a beer ball tap. You'd be surprised how often kegs get kicked and you need one of these to get the party started again."

I asked, "What if they don't have one of those party balls?"

"No problem," said Tap. "We just keep one in the trunk all iced up. Greeny works at Shop Rite and they never proof him."

As crazy as this sounded, these guys were kind of genius.

"Greeny, put on some David Lee Roth Van Halen. None of that Sammy Hagar shit for Rob!" As he reached for a new tape, I noticed that he had a rubber doll of Barney Rubble jammed into the center of his steering wheel. He was in on the joke after all. He was smiling back at me as if he knew that I would soon be as well. With that, the wicked intro to "Ain't Talkin' 'Bout Love" came blasting out of the Scirocco's speakers.

I didn't even know that much about Van Halen, but I did know that the late '80s version sounded more like Survivor than the original group. Hanging with Greeny and Tap that year I heard the entire gamut of classic rock from the backseat of that Volkswagen. From Cream to Dylan to Hendrix and everything in between, I learned why people were so passionate about this stuff. Drinking my first beers and smoking my first joints opened me up to the possibilities represented by the powerful sounds coming through the speakers.

Tap was also right about that plastic pump. It was the ticket into all the house parties I'd been missing. He even tipped me off about an after-school job stacking books at the library that gave me enough money to help pay for the eternally iced beer ball. I probably hadn't connected to music before because I hadn't experienced any of the things these bands were singing about. Getting into parties was a start. Maybe if I caught a real band in concert, I could walk by the smoking section with a shirt that proved I had earned my stripes. Then I could think about getting a girl to take off her top.

AN OBSESSION THAT'S PLEASIN'?

"DUDE, CHECK this out."

It was only a few weeks into what seemed like yet another summer for me at Camp Birchwood. The kid from the lower bunk then opened his briefcase. It was brown vinyl, but made to look like leather. There were stickers plastered all over it. These were either bands he'd seen in concert or whose shows were stacked inside. The Who, The Stones, The Police, as well as guitar gods like Eric Clapton and Carlos Santana caught my eye instantly. Some of the stickers were promos from FM stations welcoming these acts to places like Madison Square Garden, Brendan Byrne Arena, or Nassau Coliseum.

But the briefcase's exterior was nothing compared to what I saw after he flipped open those two latches. If hanging with Greeny and Tap was musically illuminating, this was fucking mind blowing. The tapes were in alphabetical order, with each artist identified by a different font. When you flipped the cassette over, you found the source of the tape and "generation" of the recording. The bands I listened to driving around in high school weren't still playing together, but this kid had recordings of them in their prime. The Doors, Led Zeppelin, David Lee Roth-era Van Halen: they were all there. I also noticed a lot of Bruce Springsteen shows. During the summer a few years before when *Born in the USA* was everywhere, I decided he wasn't worth exploring. I mentioned this to the curator of the collection.

"You need to see The Boss live. His early albums were amazing and the shows after *Darkness on The Edge Of Town* were fucking legendary,"

"So can I . . . like . . . borrow these to copy?"

"Sure, Rob. We share the same bunk bed. I'm not worried you won't give them back. But I'd prefer to do the dubbing myself."

He then reached under his bed and pulled out two single tape decks, connected by a gold-plated cable.

"They make high-speed double decks, but they can't copy for shit."

"So how can I get copies of the tapes I want?"

"Just have your parents send blanks to camp. I'd recommend Maxell XLII-90s."

As I thought about how I could get my mom to go to Crazy Eddie's and buy me a case of cassettes, I noticed about fifteen Grateful Dead shows in the middle of the collection. I was about to ask about them, but figured there was only so much I could absorb in a day.

My love of the Dead didn't take shape until later that summer, the last one I spent at Camp Birchwood. Like many Northeast summer camps, Birchwood was nestled in the Adirondack Mountains of upstate New York. The summer of '87 was my "waiter" year, which was a position of prestige at Birchwood. We were the oldest kids at the camp and all the other campers looked up to us. We also received a small paycheck for our work in the mess hall, and our parents even received a discount for the summer.

What really made being a waiter so great, however, was the freedom and privileges that came with the job. We woke up early to serve breakfast and were therefore allowed to go back to sleep while the other kids had to go to their first "period." In fact, our entire schedule was essentially voluntary. If we wanted to take out a sailboat when we were supposed to be at basketball, we could. Mostly, though, we would use that freedom to do nothing at all. The counselors were just a year or two older than we were, so we'd often get high or drunk with them during the day.

But it was the music once again that truly opened doors. I finally came to understand the genius of Springsteen's afore-mentioned *Darkness* tour, but the Dead spoke to me the most. It wasn't the beer or weed that caused me to appreciate their music, although I'm sure it made me a little more open to it. Even after hearing my counselors play them every day the previous summer, I still couldn't quite get a handle on them. Sometimes they would sound like a country band, other times blues, and sometimes I had no idea what style they were playing in. Everyone told me the only way to really appreciate the Dead was at a show. They not only allowed taping at their concerts, but even encouraged it with a special section behind the soundboard. Once again, it seemed like everyone else who appreciated it was in on some amazing inside joke. To get the best Dead tapes at Birchwood you needed to go to "Arby."

Richard Arbogast was the counselor in charge of all of Birchwood's waterfront activities. During one of my free periods, I waded down to the lake to pay him a visit. As I neared the boathouse, I heard music blasting from two speakers set up outside. I climbed the wooden stairs and got a whiff of strongest pot I had ever smelled. I knocked on the door, but it just swung open with a giant creak.

Arby had a blue bandana covering his head like a pirate. His red hair spilled out from underneath. He was leaning back in a rocking chair as I entered the room.

"Heeeeeeeeeyyyyyyyyyy . . . you're that Gross kid, right?"

"Yeah, I uh, wanted to copy a few Dead tapes from you."

"Sure. What are you into?"

I had no idea what he meant.

"There are all sorts of Dead, Rob. There's the crazy psychedelic stuff of the '60s, the countrified period of the early '70s, the intricateness of '72, and the jazzy playing of 1974."

I had no idea Arby had such an extensive vocabulary and could never imagine all these adjectives describing the same band.

"The Dead are the most documented group ever. Practically every show has been recorded by *someone*. But at the end of the day, they're just America's greatest dance band."

When I didn't respond, Arby reached under a table to grab a cassette.

"You look like a '77 guy, at least to start. Play it from 'Bertha' all the way through."

I looked at the tape in the scratched plastic case. All it said was *"Englishtown 9/3/77, II."*

I put the tape in my Walkman for my walk back to my bunk. As Arby predicted, the freight train of drums and crunchy chords that signaled the opening of "Bertha" sucked me right in. When the pianist slid his fingers across the keys, they really did sound like America's greatest dance band before they even sang a note. With the Adirondacks laid out before me, I knew I needed to hear more of this stuff. I spent the rest of the summer borrowing and copying Arby's collection after asking my parents to make a few more trips to Crazy Eddie's.

Finding the best tapes was like collecting baseball cards or comic books, except these treasures didn't lose value outside their packaging. The music within was recorded in places I'd never heard of, like Winterland Ballroom or the Fillmore East. These were foreign lands as far as I was concerned, although I was unaware at the time that the Dead had actually played in Alaska, Hawaii, and even Egypt.

They believed in magic that could only be made in the moment. It didn't happen every night, but when it did, it was more potent by far than anything that could be cooked up in a recording studio. That's why people tried to see (and tape) every show. How else could you be sure to capture the magic when it happened? Like my promise to become a Chargers fan, I had to see the Dead when they played Madison Square Garden that fall. I didn't know how I would get tickets or who I would go with, but I knew I had to be there.

Fortunately, two of my fellow waiters were getting a "Dea-ducation" at the same time I was. Arby told me about them during one of my visits to the boathouse. Stoney was a sandy-haired kid from Long Island who could funnel beers faster than any-one at Birchwood. Rose was a pint-sized kid who also lived in Westchester, although a little farther south in Scarsdale. We were drinking Genesee Lights in the camp's weight room, which was more like a gazebo with dumbbells and benches, when we decided to all go together. The "Shakedown Street" from Phila-delphia '85 was blasting while we talked.

"Some kid at my high school scalps tickets," Stoney said. "We'll just need to pay like fifty bucks to get 'em."

Rose spoke next. "But don't they only cost like eighteen fifty? That seems like a lot."

"No way," I interrupted. "We've gotta do this. I think they're playing on the weekend, so my parents will let me go. Let's drink to it."

All three of us drained our Genny Lights and knew we had a plan for that fall. However, I still hadn't met a girl. Fortunately, Birchwood had always had weekly "socials" with its sister camp across the lake. As waiters, we got daily "porch nights." If you couldn't find a girl to talk with, you'd have nothing to do for two hours. At least you could boost your confidence with Genny Lights and there was always music playing.

I was leaning against the railing one night when one of the more popular waitresses approached. Maybe the confidence I was gaining from all my new "interests" was apparent when Wendi finally introduced herself. Somehow, the fact that it was spelled with an "i" made her that much more alluring to me.

She was Jewish, as were almost all the girls at Birchwood's "sister camp," but had all the features of the classic *shiksa*. She had dirty hair, blue eyes, and the slightest sprinkling of freckles on her sun-kissed skin. Most importantly, she had the firmest set of breasts my young eyes had ever seen

"So, uh, where are you from Wendi?"

"Long Island. You're Rob, right? Where do you live?"

"Chappaqua. It's north of the city, if you know anything about Westchester."

"I don't."

I wasn't sure how to counter the resulting awkwardness, but she luckily had a solution.

"Do you want to take a walk with me?"

As we went towards the road that led back to the boys' camp, she grabbed my hand and shoved her tongue into my mouth. We kissed for a while after that and then she sent me back to my bunk walking on air. We never spoke about our feelings and she never even revealed why she came up to me. I couldn't have cared less. Almost every night we engaged in what I would later come to know as foreplay. *Animal House*, and all those awful rip-offs that followed, taught me that I had reached rarified territory. When Wendi eventually let me move my hand under the cups of her bra and later put hers inside the waistband of my boxers, I felt like my team had won the Super Bowl. Of course, I could *only assume* it felt like, given my choice of football team. My physical satisfaction was intensified by the fact that I was finally living the life I saw on the screen.

When I lost my virginity to Wendi later that summer, I naively assumed we were getting serious. The sex seemed great, but how would I be able to tell? Movies had taught me that just getting a girl was the goal. My mom always told me, "You like to put things on an imaginary shelf so you can forget about them, but that's not how life works." Maybe this was why I never considered that Wendi wasn't really that into me. I was just happy to be having sex.

Predictably, we lost touch after the summer. I was disappointed at the time, but mainly because I'd have to find another girl who'd pay attention to, let alone sleep with, me. Maybe my mom was right. At least I was going into my junior year no longer a virgin and had a Grateful Dead concert on the horizon.

SHAKEDOWN ON SEVENTH AVENUE

I COULD HARDLY contain my anticipation at school as I tried to make it through my daily schedule. It was September 18th, 1987. I never before realized how many kids had skeletons, dancing bears, or drawings of Jerry Garcia on their binders and backpacks before that day. It was no surprise that there were a lot less kids in the smoking section than usual that Friday.

I don't think any of the Deadheads at Horace Greeley High School suspected that I would be joining them that night, let alone end up attending more Dead shows than they ever did. But once I got into something, I didn't know how to do it halfway. With my short brown hair and khaki pants, I looked more like a T.G.I. Friday's employee than a guy about to see his first Grateful Dead concert. I considered the rule about not wearing the shirt of the band you were going to see, but wasn't making a conscious effort to not be a poser worse than actually being one? I didn't own a tour shirt, anyway. My magenta tie-dye commemorating Ben and Jerry's brand new "Cherry Garcia" ice cream flavor would have to do.

After spending the day squirming at my desk, I was more than ready to get the fuck out of Dodge. As soon as school ended, I drove my parents' silver Volvo GL to the Chappaqua train station. Fortunately, there was a deli across from the platform that didn't proof you for beer, so I got a six-pack of Bud for me and Rose. Stoney, who had the tickets, was meeting us at the Garden. As I waited for the train, I wondered if it would be okay to drink on the train. As soon the doors to the car opened, however, I knew there was nothing to worry about.

I would soon recognize this as the "scene" that accompanied all Grateful Dead concerts. However, it would usually be spread out over numerous parking lots, rather than a single train car. There were people smoking joints, passing around liquor bottles, and blasting tapes. I was even able to identify a few bootlegs from my growing collection. After finding a seat, I took a long gulp of my beer and waited for the train to hit Scarsdale. When it finally did, however, Rose wasn't standing in the doorway. That was okay. He must just have gotten on via another car. I wondered if they were all as wild as this one, but as soon as I saw him walking down the aisle with his mouth agape I knew the answer.

"Wow," he said. "It's a circus already."

I handed him a beer in agreement. We each polished off two more in the thirty minutes it took to get to Grand Central. As the car emptied out, we decided to walk to the Garden to temper our buzz a bit. As we reached the top of the staircase, a kid with dirty blond hair and a hooded poncho sidled up next to me. I must have given off the scent of the uninitiated since he immediately asked me if this was my first show.

"Yeah, it is."

"You're so lucky, dude. Get ready for a greeeeaaaat time."

I was lucky? I mistakenly assumed any seasoned veteran would look down on me. This was nothing like any of the high school cliques I had been exposed to. It was almost as if this kid knew what I was thinking because as he turned away he reassured me on my choice of attire.

"Cool shirt, dude. I haven't seen that one on tour."

The scene outside the Garden was similar to what I saw on the train, except it had now spilled onto the streets of Manhattan. The police were everywhere, but seemed to be observing rather than trying to control the action. It was at this point that I realized that there wasn't even a conductor to take tickets on the train. All the authority figures were hanging back tonight.

That appeared to be the only way to handle the circus on 7th Avenue. There were people selling handmade T-shirts, asking for extra tickets, and handing out flyers with the setlists from recent shows. I even saw someone selling a stack of grilled cheese sandwiches. I had no idea where or when they cooked them and didn't want to find out. In the middle of all this stood Stoney with a huge smile underneath his mop of light brown hair.

"How awesome is this?"

We didn't even need to answer as he handed us our tickets. We were in the upper deck of the Garden, but didn't care. We were even so fired up after going through the turnstiles that none of us partook as joints were passed our way upon entry. After finishing our climb to our seats, I looked at my watch. It was 8:00 PM, thirty minutes after the scheduled start. Everyone said that the Dead never began on time, anyway. This was just another way the band defied convention, which held obvious appeal.

As we waited for the lights to go down, I looked at the gear already on the stage. There was a giant rug which looked like it belonged in my grandparents' condominium. Speakers were stacked on both sides, but there were no other identifiers as to which band was playing that night. The air of anticipation inside the building made it perfectly clear that everybody knew who would be taking the stage. At about 8:30, the Garden finally went dark and a huge roar erupted. The band walked out and took what I would come to learn were their usual spots. Under us was Phil Lesh, who looked like a high school shop teacher. His glasses seemed to support his Lego-like helmet of brown hair and his rainbow tie-dye was the only evidence that he was in a band. The guy next to us assured us that, even this high up, "Phil's side always has the best sound." Bob Weir, the youngest band member and the closest thing the Dead had to a rock star, occupied the middle microphone. He was wearing black Converse hi-tops, a black T-shirt ripped around the collar, and cut-off jean shorts. This was an odd look even in 1987. Jerry Garcia occupied the last slot and wore his usual black T-shirt and corduroy pants.

I knew that the band didn't say very much to the audience. They let the music do the talking. The video footage I had seen of them suggested that they were really working on the fly. The looks the band gave each other also hinted that there were many times that they couldn't get it going at all. Luckily for us, this wasn't one of those nights.

They didn't introduce a single song, but the crowd recognized each one within a few notes. When they played, they looked like they were all soloing at once. Jerry's guitar was undoubtedly the catalyst, but he never acted like a rock star playing to a sold-out crowd. When one of his solos caused the audience to explode, his only response was to push his glasses back up the bridge of his nose. This seemed like another outlaw move to me. After all, this was the band who once tried to get Warner Brothers to let them call one of their albums *Skull Fuck*. (It was the one with the skeleton and roses on the cover.)

When the lights came on to signal the end of the first set, the first thing we saw was the guy at the end of our row snorting a line of coke off the armrest of his chair. Before we could even react, he sprung up to give us his assessment thus far:

"Hot set, but short. They're really gonna tear shit up from here on in."

He was right. When they reemerged from backstage, you could already tell that the second set was going to be where they really delivered. We all sat in the smoky darkness in anticipation as they tuned up. Jerry's fingers ran up and down his fretboard and the crowd immediately recognized "Shakedown Street." As a roar came up from the audience, both drummers erupted in what sounded like firecrackers.

WOOWWWWWWWWWWWWWHHHHHHHH!

With that, Jerry's guitar started the set in earnest. Stoney, Rose, and I stood slack-jawed as a massive spotlight panned across the crowd. This thing literally looked like the size of the Bat Signal and yet I hadn't noticed it until that moment. The song sounded like "Disco Dead" when it was recorded back in 1978, but on stage they had boiled it down to its essence. It was a funky, yet sinister, bad ass kind of a song.

But it was the version of "Morning Dew" they played about

an hour later that really made the night legendary. Jerry may have looked like Santa Claus by 1987, but he sang this ballad with all the emotion of a screaming child. You could tell by the looks of the other band members and the shrieking crowd that he didn't get this raw very often. His solo was even better, as he poured even more emotion into the notes than the words. There were times that it even sounded like the guitar cracked like a creaky voice from being played so fast. This isn't just hyperbole. This version of "Dew" is universally considered one of the best ever. The whole show was later released in the career-spanning box set that featured one concert from each of the band's 30 years.

By the time it was all over, the three of us knew we'd be back. I looked at Rose and Stoney and knew none of us were thinking about our respective train rides home. We went to more shows together, but they eventually tapered off. I, of course, couldn't exercise such moderation.

I'm glad I didn't. I saw other shows that were so good that they became live albums and others that were average or down-right disastrous. That only made the special ones better because I saw what it took to get there. I went to as many concerts as I could to maximize the chances of seeing "the one." When the band was in front of me, I knew that for one night I wouldn't have to wonder what or how they played.

However, it became about more than just the music. Dead shows gave me a sanctuary when it seemed like the real world was closing in too fast. I didn't need to worry about responsibility on tour. I could just *be*. Years later, the shows themselves became the responsibility. By that time, I was no longer taking vacations, but hiding from reality. On that Friday however, I still had 137 shows to go. I boarded the train to Chappaqua only thinking about the next one and how I was going to track down a tape of what I'd just experienced.

ADRIFT BUT NOT ALONE

"SO WHAT YOU really need to do is develop trust in your classmates. This is why it's so important to establish it in by falling back into their arms."

It was my second day of Freshman Orientation at the University of Rochester. We had already herded into the covered field house for a series of activities normally seen at corporate retreats. Now we were forced to endure this "team building" game called the trust fall. Luckily, the "orientators" moved on to another senseless scenario before I had to ask a total stranger to keep me from falling backwards onto the Astroturf of the school's field house.

"Okay, who here has heard of a 'focus ring?'"

These super-perky upperclassmen in matching Rochester polo shirts and khaki shorts then started pulling ropes out of a circle with a tennis ball in the middle. We were already in a concentric circle, so all they had to do was hand a rope to each of us.

"Now you are all the spokes of our 'wheel.'"

They placed a tennis ball in the center and our task was to pull on the "spokes" to place the ball onto a pedestal. The goal was to slide the ring down the pedestal, which was even more phallic than it sounds, if you can believe that. I still have no idea how this would help incoming freshmen adjust to college life. It seemed to me that the Class of '93 was just happy being away from their parents. The questions asked by the orientation staff were almost as asinine as the activities themselves.

"What do you see as your biggest obstacle toward adjusting to college?"

"How do you think you will need support to overcome them?"

I desperately wished to be back inside the four cinder block walls of my dorm room. Thankfully, I heard some much-needed chatter near the doorway.

"Psst! Freshman! Come here!"

I didn't know if they were even talking to me. I'm sure there were many other first-year students stuck in that circle who would have bitten off their own arm to escape. Maybe I looked especially disenchanted or possibly my T-shirt made me an attractive candidate for extraction. I was wearing one with the Dead's iconic skull and lightning bolt logo in the center that read, "If you have to ask, you wouldn't understand." I had picked it up in the parking lot at Giants Stadium the previous year and it had been in my constant rotation ever since.

This guy with brown curly hair and beard was offering me a lifeline. I would later learn that his fraternity nickname was Shaggy. He wore a tie-dye shirt and sandals, which confirmed that it had been my shirt which caught his attention.

"Dude, this thing sucks, huh?"

"Definitely," I replied.

"You wanna grab a few beers with some much cooler people?"

Those were all the words I needed to hear. I quickly got off the Astroturf and walked out into the August sunshine. Waiting for me in front of a black Pontiac Firebird were four of the most dissimilar guys I could have imagined. It was like that scene in every heist movie when you meet the "the crew." If each of these guys had some special skill, however, I couldn't imagine what it was.

"Dolf" was a blond, blue-eyed mountain. He was wearing an old army helmet and had a grin like Muttley from the *Laff-a-Lympics* show. "Mustafa" appeared to be of Middle Eastern descent and had the beginnings of an impressive beard developing. Someone had nicknamed him after one of the terrorists in Chuck Norris' *Delta Force*, but it was hardly out of prejudice. These guys didn't seem to discriminate against anybody. "Anvil," obviously named ironically, was a Filipino who looked like he barely weighed a hundred pounds. Anvil would eventually be the first person I ever knew to come out of the closet. When he finally did, not only was no one surprised, but no one actually cared. As I suspected, the brothers of Lambda Sigma Delta (appropriately abbreviated LSD) were nothing if not accepting.

"Hollywood" was so normal looking that I wondered if he'd just been recruited for the afternoon as well. I couldn't imagine what he could possibly have in common with the rest of the group. He wore a grey tweed blazer and black mock turtleneck with a pair of blue corduroys. On anyone else, this ensemble would look like the contents of a Goodwill donation bin, but he had the confidence to pull it off. Not surprisingly, he addressed me first after I showed up on the scene.

"You wanna come with us to get Stones tickets?"

He handed me a can of Old Milwaukee that I immediately sucked down. Without knowing it, I was already rushing a fraternity. Later, I would also meet a Squiggy, Scooby, Lumpy, Spanky, and Ozzy. When I showed my parents the fraternity's formal composite photo after coming home for winter break, they joked that they sounded like the Seven Dwarfs' evil cousins.

In the car on the way to the record store that housed the nearest Ticketmaster, the "Delts" regaled me with some tales from the previous school year. As beers and bowls were passed, I instantly knew that this was where I belonged. With my afternoon buzz intensifying, I tried to find out more about these guys and how to join them.

"What kinds of things does your fraternity do when you're not just hanging out?"

Hollywood fielded my question. "We don't really participate in the standard fraternity events the school puts on. We did win the inter-fraternity basketball tournament, however, thanks to Shaggy over here."

"Shaggy?" I had just met him, but couldn't imagine him owning a pair of sneakers, let alone shooting a basketball.

"Oh yeah, Shag took a couple of hits of acid about a half hour before tip-off of the opening game. On our possession, the shit really starts to kick in. He pulls up for a wide-open jumper and the ball goes straight up and lands at his feet. After that, though, he couldn't miss. The guy scored 40 points!"

College had just gotten a hell of a lot more interesting.

LIVE MORE, THINK LESS

LAMBDA SIGMA DELTA defied convention, which was what drew me to it. It still shared some customs with other fraternities, including the one I knew from *Animal House*. We had to wear pledge pins, clean up after parties, and have spontaneous "line-ups." Lineups occurred when the brothers pulled you out of bed in the middle of the night and made you answer trivia questions about the history of the fraternity. Wrong answers meant you had to do a shot of Fighting Cock bourbon. Of course, these were the last days before 911 calls and lawsuits that would make an upper-classman approaching graduation at least think twice about forcing some kid they'd just met to drink a glass of 103-proof whiskey.

The only reason I ever got the punishment shots was when the brothers got bored one night of my endless string of correct answers. My mind for minutiae (or just my OCD) made me able to remember all that stuff no matter how much I drank.

"Jesus, Gross, just get back in line. You can have a shot if you feel like it."

I hadn't imbibed much bourbon before college, but took a liking to it almost immediately. At first it burned like hell, but soon a warm glow spread throughout my body. Later in the lineup, they asked me if I wanted to do a punishment shot for one of my pledge brothers. When it was clear that the whiskey wasn't a punishment for me, the brothers upped the ante to a triple shot. After getting it all down, my entire face contorted as I waited for what I thought was the inevitable "reversal of fortune."

"Uh, guys, I think we need to find a new punishment for this kid. For the next lineup, he's only getting shots of milk."

That was the last thing I remembered before blacking out.

When I came to, my head was throbbing so hard I figured I had to be bleeding. My pillow was drenched with drool and my shirt was off. I never slept topless, so I instantly knew shit must have gotten really out of control. My university-issued phone was blinking like a neon billboard that demanded I listen to my voicemail. There were six messages, each one more urgent than the last.

"Yo, uh, Rob . . . This is Squirrel, your big brother. We were just making sure that you got back to your dorm okay."

"Rob, it's Squirrel again. You had a ton of shots and the brothers want to know you're alright."

"Rob, you need to get in touch with us."

The other three were from the president of the Phi Gamma sorority, housed in the dorm next to mine.

"Yes, I'm trying to get in touch with Rob Gross. You ran through our hall last night at about 2:00 AM and woke all the sisters up. As angry as the girls were, they were mostly worried because you were really, *really*, drunk."

Her tone was so polite, she sounded like a telemarketer. I wondered how she got my number until I heard her final sentence:

"You also left your Grateful Dead shirt tied to my front door. It had your name on it."

The shirts I brought to Birchwood every summer were still marked with a Sharpie laundry pen. I was far beyond the age of name tags, but I didn't want to lose any of those cool shirts I'd been acquiring.

Now my neuroses had really fucked me since I wouldn't be able to deny whatever I'd done. When I went to pick up the shirt, the president seemed to feel more pity towards me than anger.

When she untied it from her door, she noticed that my pledge pin was still stuck in it.

"Rob, as an executive board member, I know how serious losing your pledge pin is. You need to be careful."

As I eagerly took the shirt from her, I humbly muttered that I understood.

"I don't just mean about the pledge pin. You have to pace yourself in college. The sisters thought it was funny to have a guy topless running through the hallway in the middle of the night."

"Oh, good," I replied.

"But it's not funny. Don't you see that?"

I was so relieved to come out of my first blackout seemingly unscathed that I didn't really see her point. Otherwise, I'd have seen that she was talking about even more than just the drinking. It didn't help that the brothers hailed me as a hero for surviving the night. I'm sure they were also a little relieved that I didn't need to have my stomach pumped or something.

Scoring points with them made me feel good. I really wanted to become a part of this group. The brotherhood seemingly contained all types. There were jocks, nerds, burnouts, ladies' men, and guys I couldn't even categorize. The guys in the house weren't all Deadheads, but they were all open to the type of adventure the Dead's music represented. Like the band itself, each guy in the fraternity was a misfit in one way or another. Somehow, however, it all came together.

Among my pledge class I was the only one who regularly attended Dead shows. This did not escape the attention of the brothers during Hell Week. During it, they forced us to listen to entire cassette sides of the most maddening sounds imaginable, like 45 minutes' worth of Billy Joel's "We Didn't Start the Fire." It didn't even stop with bad music. Another tape had 90-minutes of someone just playing Pac-Man. They must have hooked up a gaming system and recorded it through the tape deck in the fraternity's lounge. We were allowed to eat and sleep the minimum amount to keep us alive, but I at least had to give the brothers credit for their creativity. After we heard the Pac-Man tape the third time, however, I foolishly asked the pledge master if we could hear something else.

"This is the highest score ever gotten within these walls and you're experiencing it *as it happened*. It's a pivotal moment in Lambda Sigma Delta history! You don't want to deprive your fellow pledges of that, do you?"

"I, uh, guess not . . ."

"We do have an alternative, Gross. The brothers made this one especially for you."

For a second, I actually thought I might be getting some sort of reward. That's how naïve and exhausted I was.

The opening bars to the Dead's "Scarlet Begonias" began, and I felt better than I had all week. But right before Jerry was about to sing, the tape stopped.

Wakawakawakawaka . . . Fucking Pac-Man went on for another fifty-five minutes.

"We even broke out the 110-minute tape for you. Dontcha like it? It gives you an extra 10 minutes per side!"

Our pledge master was nicknamed Dagwood. I don't think anyone even knew his real name. By 1990 he must have been the last preppy standing, a townie from Rochester, always in a button-down and loafers, even if he was wearing shorts. If fraternity life really was *Animal House*, he'd be cast as an Omega. Yet he was the most subversive Delt of all, which was why he was pledge master. He was the one who showed me Hunter S. Thompson's first book, *Hell's Angels*. He even had tapes of Thompson's drunken college lectures from the '70s. Thompson said on them that the Angels weren't worth the hype because they weren't smart, funny, or brave. "Be an outlaw, but do it your own way and for your own reasons." Sage advice, even if I was still figuring out how to put it to use.

Besides finding inventive ways to torture pledges, Dagwood was notable for the ducktail of hair that practically ran into his collar. He called it his "Partyometer," since the higher it rose off his neck the better the time he was having. He and some of the older brothers liked to drink off campus on Thursdays when fraternities hadn't yet started throwing their weekend blowouts, which LSDs called "amateur hour." Their own parties were the obvious exception. In the bars you had to be 21 or have a fake ID to get in, which made the crowd more selective. Fortunately, I still had mine from high school. Unfortunately, Dagwood was the only one willing to drive me back to campus. Those rides home with my pledge master blind drunk behind the wheel made me think that stories like Hunter Thompson's might have actually happened.

He drove a 1989 Ford Crown Victoria because "that's what the cops drive." The car was dubbed "The Gunner," because the tape deck would eat any cassette that wasn't Guns N' Roses. More specifically, the car would chew up any tape but their eight-song 1988 EP, *Lies*. Later we would discover that *Use Your Illusion II*, but not *I*, could survive destruction in The Gunner. Dagwood once mentioned that it would also accept Johnny Cash's *Live at Folsom Prison*, although I never witnessed it personally.

It was as if The Gunner knew what music had enough balls to pass muster. Just like its owner, the car survived on its gut instincts alone. It seemed that the less attention Dagwood paid to the road, the better he drove. He kept his seat leaned so far back that he was practically lying on his back. I couldn't get a reading on the Partyometer even if I wanted to in that position. While Axl Rose belted out a full-throttle cover of Aerosmith's "Mama Kin," Dagwood shared with me his secrets.

"Gross, I call you 'Gross.' There are no pledge nicknames in 'The Gunner.' I don't know why people get in accidents when there's so much room on the road."

As he said this, he would turn the steering wheel to both sides to illustrate his point. While he giggled his ass off, I wondered how he hadn't ever been pulled over. One night I was drunk enough to actually ask him myself.

"Well, Gross, it did happen once. The cops were sure I was fucked up and they were right. I was drunk *and* tripping my face off."

I was captivated. "How'd you pull it off?"

"They threw every test at me. I walked in a straight line, I touched my nose, and even passed the breathalyzer. That surprised me, although maybe I didn't all have that much to drink due to the potency of the acid."

"What did they do next?"

"After the breathalyzer, they were so pissed. They knew I wasn't even close to being sober and couldn't prove it. Eventually, they just gave up and asked me if *I* thought I should be driving."

"Holy shit," I said. "What did you say to them?"

"'Officer, I do believe that's a judgment call.'"

That must have been the most inflammatory statement of all. The cops really had no recourse, when you thought about it. That was, unless they could legally introduce a Partyometer reading into evidence during the trial.

ONE MORE SATURDAY NIGHT

EVEN BEFORE I began rushing LSD, I had heard about the parties. As pledges, we had to tend bar at every one. It was supposed to be one of our many demeaning responsibilities, but felt like more of a privilege. Working the taps on those Saturday nights put you in the center of everything. It meant that girls would talk to you, if only because you stood between them and the beer. In 1990, that meant Old Milwaukee, but you would have thought we were dispensing Cristal due to the massive crowds pushing up against the bar.

It was the first time in my life that I didn't need an excuse to talk to girls. Sometimes, they'd even initiate the conversation. This happened at my first "One-Piece Party." It was LSD's biggest party of the year. The only requirement for admission was that you could only wear one piece of clothing, with no exceptions. I had opted for a Grateful Dead tapestry tied around my waist, but other brothers were a little more daring. One brother wore an apron, another a strategically placed sock, and my roommate wore only his hat with Lambda Sigma Delta embroidered on it.

I had just finished my bar shift when a girl with crimped blond hair started talking to me. "You don't look like a Delt with the short hair and all . . ."

There were plenty of pledges and brothers that didn't have long hair, so I wasn't sure why that was worth mentioning.

"You look like more of a soccer player or something."

The Delt in the hat happened to be my roommate. "Ice" was also from Westchester. As a pledge, I could now live in the fraternity's on-campus housing as long as it was with a brother. LSD didn't have a house, but rather a floor with four narrow hallways running off the main lounge.

By the time my shift behind the bar was done, Ice had already found a girl to take back to our room. However, I only realized this after I started making progress with the girl I had been speaking with.

She asked if we could go somewhere to talk, but the way she said "talk" made it clear that she wasn't interested in conversation. My eyes scanned the lounge, which was a sea of debauchery. I saw a group of girls from the predominantly Jewish sorority passing a joint to one of the brothers. In another corner I saw Lurch, who was really *that tall*, holding up a 3-beer funnel. Another brother, Sponge, was quickly tightening the valve to keep it sealed. Nirvana's "About A Girl" wailed from the speakers. This was right before everybody knew about them, which the best time to get into a band.

"Uh, yeah. We can probably go to my room," I feebly replied.

"That's so cool. You get to live in the fraternity."

She was right, except when you weren't sure if your roommate had locked you out. I hoped like hell that he hadn't. This was my first promising female prospect since the school year had started. I had fooled around with a few girls in the corner of the lounge or in the hallways, but hadn't slept with anyone. I mentioned this fact to Ice before the party and he told me not to stress it.

"Dude, you'll find that hex-breaker. That's the best part of being a Delt. You never know when or where your next sex is coming from."

I never thought of that being a *good* thing before. But while I contemplated this, I noticed that my friend from the bar was staring intently at my crotch. I didn't think she was *that* into me. Maybe Ice was right, maybe luck was around the corner. It was then that I remembered that I was basically wearing a kilt with no underwear. Now I understood why girls crossed their legs so tightly. Even with all the booze flowing through me, I was a little embarrassed. But the girl sitting across from me was now giggling.

"You said you live here on the floor?"

I felt a sigh of relief when I turned the knob to my room. When I turned around, we were suddenly making out. As we stumbled through the doorway, I blurted out that I didn't even know her name.

"It's Jacqui, with a *c* and *q*."

Before I could introduce myself, she shoved me onto the bed. It was right about the time she started to blow me that I heard rustling from the other side of the room. Ice didn't even have sheets on his bed, just an old sleeping bag. As a result, the sound was unmistakable; he was in there. I could only hope that he at least wasn't conscious. There was no stopping now. The only light in the room was what was seeping under the door from the hallway. Over Jacqui's bramble of hair, I couldn't have seen anything on Ice's side even if I'd wanted to.

And I definitely didn't want to.

Jacqui picked her head up and asked if I had protection. Fortunately, I had a box of condoms behind my CD player. Things had moved so quickly that I didn't even put on music. I could hear the lounge blasting James Brown's "Sex Machine," which seemed perversely appropriate. "Just tell me what you want," she purred.

"I'm not sure what you mean."

"I mean, what you want me to do?"

I couldn't believe my ears. Just getting laid was good enough, although I was really tempted to tell her she could help clean up Ice's side of the room.

"This is good," I slurred.

It was a good thing that Jacqui got on top of me, as I was too drunk to move. I couldn't imagine I was a particularly good lay. Once again, I didn't consider the feelings of the person I was having sex with. I was just happy to be doing it and felt a much-needed surge of confidence. I couldn't tell if she was disappointed in my performance or was just experiencing the awkwardness that comes with a one-night stand, but she just stood up and got dressed almost immediately afterwards. I couldn't bother trying to navigate my tapestry/kilt again, so I quickly grabbed a pair of boxers. This way I could at least say goodbye and rejoin the party with appropriate attire.

I tried to push through my inebriation to catch her before she left. As I went through the doorway, I spotted her turning the corner to go down the stairs. As disappointment was about to kick in, I heard Ice's voice over my shoulder.

"Told ya. You never know where it's coming from next."

JUST RIDE

JUST WHEN I THOUGHT the fraternity had shown me every possible archetype, I'd meet someone completely different. Take Money, a fast-talking kid from Brooklyn who loved hip-hop but also dropping acid. He was the one who gave me the pledge nickname of "Luca Brasi." I had never mentioned during rush my love of *The Godfather* (like *Animal House*, there isn't a wasted moment on screen), so I asked him why he gave it to me. He told me that the fraternity "just needed a Luca."

I was honored to have the name, even if I was nothing like the enforcer of the Corleone clan. "That's not the point," he said. "You gotta make it your own."

"It sounds like you're talking about more than my nickname," I said.

"Bet."

I always wondered how he ended up a Delt, but didn't have the nerve to ask. Instead, I asked him why he loved tripping so much. I figured it was almost the same thing and I was legitimately curious. Even with all the Dead shows I'd been seeing, I hadn't yet tried psychedelics myself.

"I never tried it back in Brooklyn, but my philosophy is to say yes to anything. With acid, you feel like something amazing is about to happen. Isn't that what it's all about? Listen, Luca, the guys I live with have a party almost every other weekend. You won't hear any *Jerry* or anything, but I think you might get into it. I think you'd get down with the different vibe."

He said "Jerry" like it was a bad word, but I was intrigued. Money lived in a suite with three university athletes who were all twice my size. I couldn't imagine what they were like when they partied.

A few weeks later, I got a voicemail message:

"Yo, Luca . . . Money. This is your shout out for Friday. You don't need to bring anything, although you might want to grab a *forty*."

I knew nothing about malt liquor, so I bought the one at the front of the mini-mart cooler before the party. It was a Schlitz with the blue bull on the label. I decided to drink it on the way and it didn't take long for me to feel its potency.

By the time I got to the suite, I had a pretty heavy buzz. I could feel the bass thumping through the wooden door when I knocked. I would soon recognize this as Curtis Mayfield's "Super Fly" by way of the Beastie Boys' "Egg Man." When the door opened, I found myself looking right into the chest of the school's star pitcher.

"Uh, Money invited me. My name's Rob."

"Rob? He didn't mention it."

"Maybe he used the name *Luca*?"

Suddenly, his face lit up. Maybe I was making the name my own after all.

"Fuck! Luca! Yeah, he said you were coming by. I'm Rucker. Come on in. Shit's just starting to get crazy."

I could already smell the weed. That was nothing new. But quickly scanning the suite, I realized that this was nothing like an LSD party. As diverse as the fraternity was, we still attracted mostly white kids. I was suddenly not only looking at all sorts of ethnicities, but they were dancing in a way I'd never seen. Bumping, grinding, writhing, whatever you want to call it, these people were seriously feeling the music. Up on one of the tables, I spotted Money face to face with a pretty Latina. Their shoulders, arms, and legs all appeared to be moving at once. Every so often, they'd turn their heads, which was when I first got his attention. He smiled and jumped off the table, leaving his dance partner mid-step.

"Luca, *noyce!*"

He led me down the hallway towards the source of the music.

"Money, your suitemates are fucking *huge!*"

"Who, you mean Rucker? Yeah, he plays baseball. The other two guys who live with me play football, but they're cool."

He pointed to two guys both wearing jean shorts and tank tops. As I looked back and forth, I quickly realized that they were identical twins. Apparently, Rich and Jason hailed from some small town outside of Syracuse and lived for these parties. Even though it was only a little after 11:00 PM, they were already bombed. All these athletes belonged to the "jock house," but chose not to live in the fraternity. "They love the vibe here," Money told me.

I was starting to see why. Behind the stereo, there was a 300-pound guy in overalls cutting into a party ball with a Bowie Knife. The Coors Light box it came in was at his feet and ice was scattered on the floor. There was a crowd gathered around him. For a second, I thought he might try to drink the whole thing. All I could lamely offer up was that it "looked like an interesting project."

"Thanks, dude. I'm a surgeon."

"You should have been at our last suite party," Money chimed in. "We just rode up and down one of their hall's elevators with the beer ball. Every time the elevator stopped, that was another person added to the party. Before you knew it, campus security was trying to shut it down."

I didn't even think LSD would come up with something that spontaneous. I took another long pull on my malt liquor and spotted African-American guys who looked about fifty.

"How do guys like that even *get* here?"

"You know, Luca, word gets around."

At this point, two guys with high-top fades started walking towards us. I instantly tensed up, but once they screamed out *"Mon-eh!,"* I knew it was okay. He asked me if I was cool being on my own for a bit.

"Sure. What kind of shit could I really get into?"

Within seconds of his leaving, another huge guy in a crew cut started talking to me. "Are you a brother?"

He must have thought I was in the fraternity with some of Money's suitemates.

"Uh, yeah."

"You are? So what's your house look like then?"

I couldn't resist fucking with him.

"It's off white, stucco—pretty average sized for Westchester."

The second the words left my mouth I knew where things were going.

"Listen, dickhead. I know who you are. You're a Delt. I can't believe you guys even party here."

"Well, Money's a Delt . . ."

"My girlfriend last year went to that one-piece party you guys have. After that, she fuckin' broke up with me. God knows what you guys did to her."

I really didn't appreciate the insinuation. "Dude, I'm pretty sure all the hooking up at the one-piece is consensual. Maybe your girlfriend just met someone there and liked what she saw."

Even with the malt liquor numbing me, I felt the guy's finger instantly ramming into my sternum.

"What did you fucking say?"

"I, uh . . ."

Before I could finish my sentence, he'd knocked me to the ground.

As I started to pick myself off the floor, I realized how drunk I was. I felt like the party came to a screeching halt. I was sure the music had stopped.

"It's Luca! Don't worry, we got your back!"

I looked up to see Rucker, the twins, and Money all running towards me. From Money, I might have expected this kind of support. At least we were in the same fraternity. The twins quickly grabbed my assailant and ushered him towards the door. When they returned, they told me how impressed they were that I had gotten into trouble so quickly.

"Luca, man, you're a fuckin' bad ass! What'd you say to that guy?"

"I don't know. He was just giving me shit because his ex-girlfriend had a good time at one of our parties. Apparently, it was *too* good a time for him."

"Dude, you defended your brothers. Nice job."

"Yeah, but isn't that guy one of *your* brothers?"

"He is, but he's kind of a dick. If you're friends with Money, we know you're all right."

I told Money no one had ever told me they had my back. I hadn't even heard that expression before.

"Luca, there's more out there than the fraternity. You probably wonder how I ended up joining. A lot of people do. It's not that complicated. I just met some cool guys who asked me to pledge. But you gotta stay open to all the possibilities. That's why I live with these guys. The fraternity can't be your entire life, even if it's one as cool as ours."

I pounded the last third of my malt liquor and asked him the obvious question:

"So when's the next suite party?"

DON'T WORRY ABOUT THE DESTINATION

MY GROWING CONFIDENCE allowed me to hook up with a few girls, without anything becoming serious. They didn't seem to expect anything from me afterwards and I was more than okay with that. It felt great knowing I didn't need to have a relationship with every girl I slept with. I wouldn't have had any idea how to make one work, anyway.

I figured Kerry McNaughton would just be another one of those girls. Sleeping with her that fall just felt like two college kids having fun—until it didn't. She waitressed at an Irish pub off-campus and we started talking over a few nights at the bar. We didn't have any deep conversations, but I instantly felt comfortable with her. I wasn't even thinking about hooking up with her and probably revealed a lot more of myself as a result. She was pretty, but not in the earthy brunette way I usually went for. She wore her brown hair at shoulder length, and her fair skin made her pale blue eyes that much more striking.

She was your classic Irish Catholic, but her faith was more of a cultural characteristic than a religious one. This was one of the things we seemed to have in common. When she invited me back to her apartment after a few nights spent talking at the bar, it felt like a natural progression of things. Nonetheless, I had no expectations.

She lived just a few blocks away, so there wasn't any time for me to get stuck inside my own head. She immediately poured us both glasses of Jameson and put on some music. The whiskey tasted a hell of a lot better than the stuff we drank at the fraternity. From the speakers, I heard young girls screaming from a crowd as a guy talked about buying a Japanese guitar. It sounded like Cheap Trick's *Budokan* album, but I'd never heard this song. Kerry told me "Can't Hold On" was left off the original release, but on an EP. Now she really had my attention as the band somehow infused a ballad meant for a speakeasy with the "power pop" sound they popularized.

Kerry went on to talk about growing up in Buffalo with two older brothers. "They taught me how to hold my whiskey," she revealed. She also wanted to know things about me, which made me even more interested in her.

"You like football, Rob?"

I didn't expect that one. "Actually, I've been a San Diego Chargers fan since I was a kid." I figured I'd have to explain my choice of team.

"So you grew up loving Dan Fouts or something?"

I was understandably floored, but tried not to let on. I was trying to play it cool with a girl I thought I had no interest in.

"Yeah, uh, that's pretty much it. You a fan?"

"I'm from Buffalo, what do *you* think?"

"Oh yeah," I said. "They've made the Super Bowl the last two years."

"That has nothing to do with it, although it sucks we didn't win either time. In my house, Sundays are all about football. No matter what else is going on, we're either at the stadium or in front of the TV."

"What's the tailgate situation like?"

"It's kind of a free-for-all. It reminds me of seeing the Dead at Rich Stadium."

I didn't even touch that subject. I was already hooked, but not just because of the things she was talking about. Her confidence really drew me in. Somehow it felt like we were talking about more than just football and music. I had never felt a connection like this with a girl.

We ended up sleeping together that night. It was the first time that the act itself didn't seem so important to me. It was also the first time I really paid attention to the person I was having sex with. When I looked into Kerry's eyes, I knew something was happening. I wasn't sure what it was, but the intensity of it was a little frightening. It certainly didn't fit into the world I had created since coming to Rochester.

As I result, I felt relieved when Kerry announced that she was driving me back to the fraternity. I wouldn't have to worry about what the sex meant.

The next time we slept together, it was more intense. Afterwards, I thought she might invite me to stay. When she instead told me that I was going back to LSD, I didn't feel that same sense of relief. The next time we had sex, I was truly disappointed when she told me she was driving me back. I thought it about bringing it up, but wanted to be sure of what I was feeling before I tried to do something about it. It seemed like the less she seemed to care about what these nights meant, the more I did. The fact that I had never felt like this made it harder to be sure if it was real or not.

After we slept together for the fourth time, I couldn't hold back my feelings.

"Kerry, why don't I just crash here? It's not like I'm going to make my early class."

"I'd prefer it if I take you back to the fraternity.""What if I don't *want* to go? Shouldn't I have a say in this?" It suddenly felt like we were talking about more than where I would spend the next few hours sleeping.

"Rob, the fraternity is where you want to be. It's your whole world . . . besides the Dead and the Chargers, I guess." Her tone revealed that she didn't see this as a positive.

"Why is that such a bad thing? I'm myself at LSD. They don't expect anything else from me."

"They might not," she responded. "But maybe *you* should. You're in your junior year. I don't think you're as free as you think you are."

I didn't know what she was talking about. Maybe this conversation was a bad idea. Yeah, I was in my junior year and didn't want to be tied down. I was just taking off. What was so wrong with that?

"I don't know what you have against the fraternity."

"That's not it, Rob. I actually used to date a fraternity guy when I was a freshman. It felt like it might become something serious. I went to the parties and used to hang around and wait."

I had no idea she'd ever had anything remotely close to a boyfriend. Kerry acted like she was so above the whole college scene. She had a job and her own apartment.

"*Wait* for what?"

"I don't know, maybe for him to come back to my room just once. Or maybe to at least pretend I meant as much as his fraternity."

I wondered which fraternity it was and who had hurt her so

badly. Before I could open up that can of worms, she grabbed her car keys to leave. I knew this conversation, and what it could lead to, was now over.

We didn't see each other for a while after that. I stopped going to the bar she worked at without even realizing it. I now knew her "cool chick" persona was somewhat of a defense mechanism, just like my sarcasm. Of course, she was accusing me of using the fraternity in the same way. Who the fuck did she think she was? It's not like I'd treated her like all the other girls I met so far in college. I listened. I shared things about myself.

Soon, Kerry made a point of not coming anywhere near LSD. The one time we accidentally bumped into each other was at another fraternity's party. I was pretty drunk and elected to pretend that all the time that had passed since we saw each other last was accidental.

"These guys don't really know how to throw a good party. Why don't we go back to your apartment like we used to?"

She immediately shot that idea down.

"Don't even bother trying to act like you're interested, Rob. If you really wanted to see me, you would have reached out a long time ago."

I was not expecting this conversation, especially given my state of inebriation.

"Kerry, it wasn't just me that got us here. You talked all this shit about the fraternity. Maybe you're just bitter about whatever happened between you and that guy."

That was all she needed to hear before she ran out the door.

March Winds Blow Through Nassau

SEEING ALL THOSE DEAD SHOWS during school meant that I didn't have typical college vacations. At least I never had to scramble for spring break plans. For instance, 1992's spring tour took me from Atlanta to Hampton, Washington, and Long Island. My itinerary included flights, rental cars, and a stop at my parents' house before heading out to the Nassau Coliseum shows. Beforehand, I celebrated my 21st birthday at the Capital Centre outside of DC. Deadheads always claimed that if you mailed a photocopy of your driver's license along with your ticket request, you'd be rewarded with great seats. I had been drinking on a fake ID since high school, but it was nice to be able to leave it in the car as I sat nine rows from the stage.

After crashing in a nearby hotel, I took off the following morning for Chappaqua. My parents were taking me out for dinner at my favorite Mexican restaurant for my birthday. Unfortunately, there was a message on my parents' answering machine from the Delt who was supposed to go with me to the first Nassau show. He had family plans that he couldn't get out of. He was from Manhattan and his parents wanted to take him out to dinner. It wasn't his birthday or anything, but I couldn't really be mad. I was a little disappointed and not sure who to ask to the show. My mom must have overheard me on the kitchen phone when I got the news.

"Why don't you ask your father to go with you?"

I wasn't prepared for her suggestion.

"I mean, I can always get someone. It's the first show of the run and I'm sure a lot of people would love to go."

"That's not the point. You think he took you to all those games when you were younger because he loves football? Who takes you every time the Chargers play in New York?"

"But how do you know he'd even *want* to go?"

"Just ask him, please."

Sure enough, she was right. His face lit up when I invited him. I also got the sense he and my mom might have discussed it beforehand. It was a cool March day, so I didn't know how much of a scene there would be in the parking lot. It would really be just about attending the show.

"Just treat it like any other one of your concerts. I'll buy us some sandwiches," he assured me.

Like any other concert? I had no idea how to do that. After he loaded up my cooler with two Italian subs and a six-pack of Becks, we took off for Long Island. While he drove, I tried to give him a crash course on what he might see that night. I played him a tape from the previous tour to get him up to speed.

"I've heard their music before, Rob. It's been coming out of your room for years. It usually sounds like one long song, though. They don't take breaks or announce what they're playing?"

"They don't stop when they're jamming. Everybody knows what they're playing after a few notes, anyway."

"Jamming?"

This was going be a little harder than I thought.

"Maybe it'll make sense when they're on stage playing."

By the time we got to the Coliseum, the weather was pretty raw. The wind was whipping through the parking lot, so we decided to sit in the open trunk of my parents' Subaru GL station wagon. It felt like we were in a luxury box seat for the Grateful Dead parking lot scene. Sitting side by side, it was cramped yet warm.

"So what do you usually do before the show?"

"When it's not freezing, I might explore the lot."

"What for?"

"I usually buy a beer, a shirt, or something to eat."

"We have all that here, though. Plus, you have so many shirts."

"Yeah, but the ones in the lot change depending on the tour. As for the food, where else are you going to get 'Rasta Pasta?'"

He started laughing and said, "I guess you're right."

I was about to continue trying to explain the normal pre-show scene, when a kid in a Mexican pancho and knit hat with braided tassels approached our car.

"You guys need any doses?"

"No, we're set. We've both got sandwiches," he replied.

The kid was so confused that he just stared at us in disbelief. Of course, he was clearly tripping his brains out as well. All I wanted was for him to move on to another car before I had to explain to my dad that he wanted to sell us acid. But before I could respond, my dad asked him if he wanted one of our beers.

"Absolutely," he said.

My dad pulled one out of the cooler for him.

His eyes got even wider when he saw the label. "Becks, an import."

He asked my dad if he'd seen any other shows on the tour.

"No, but you might want to talk to my son. He's the expert."

I couldn't believe how proud my father sounded saying that. I'd always assumed he viewed my love of the Dead as an annoyance.

"Dude, you brought your dad to the show? That's actually pretty cool."

I was starting to realize how right he was. Our new friend finished his beer and told us to have a good show. I looked down at my watch and realized it was time to head in. As we walked toward the gate, my dad put his hand on my shoulder.

"He seemed like a nice kid, don't you think?"

I just had to smile. My dad sweetly saw the good in things. I could only hope I got some of that from him.

"Yeah, Dad. He did."

For once, I didn't really care what songs the band picked that night or how they played them. They opened with an appropriately selected "Cold Rain & Snow." When they played "It's All Over Now," my dad proudly told me he recognized the song as a cover from the Rolling Stones' early days.

"This isn't so wild, Rob. I don't know what I was expecting."

I told him to reserve judgment until the second set. "That's when the songs get a lot longer."

During the set-opening jam from "China Cat Sunflower" into "I Know You Rider," the band really caught fire. As the roar of the crowd built, he looked over at me. He had to scream for me to hear.

"I think I kind of get it!" Once again, I couldn't believe how proud he sounded. What I thought was going to be a chore turned out to be amazing. When things eventually did get a little too spacey for him, he just sat down. But he was tapping his feet the whole time, even during the drum solo. As if to reward him, the band played more covers by the Stones, Chuck Berry, and Bob Dylan to close things out. His review of the show confirmed how much he had enjoyed himself.

"They're basically just a dance band, except for that psychedelic stuff. Also, I haven't smelled that much pot since I took your mother to that bluegrass festival."

My dad was full of surprises.

After the houselights came on, we started putting on our jackets for the cold walk back to the car. I spotted a guy with a tape recorder walking up the stairs. He took one look at us and asked if we were father and son. When I said yes, he told us he was from *Newsday*.

"Was this your father's first Grateful Dead concert?" "Absolutely," I said.

The reporter pointed the microphone at my dad. "That's pretty amazing for you to come out on a night like this just for him."

"That's just it," my dad said. "I think he *thought* I was coming for him, but I think it ended up being more for me."

We never found out whether we made the article, but the best part was that I don't think either of us cared.

THE PROPER POTION

THE UNIVERSITY OF ROCHESTER, like most colleges, has its own annual spring party weekend. "Dandelion Day" is admittedly a pretty lame thing to call it, but it was the most raging party of the year. "D-Day" was also the day that a large percentage of students ate psychedelic mushrooms. As that last Saturday in April approached, kids who would were normally too timid to even smoke weed were scrambling to track down an eighth of 'shrooms.

"It's actually all-natural," was the word around campus. No one mentioned that they were usually grown in cow shit. I thought taking mushrooms on "D-Day" was a total cliché, and was also still not ready to take hallucinogens. I knew myself well enough to know that letting my mind get that open might not be a good idea. I was always up for beers, bowls, or shots, but the buzz I got from them felt somewhat controllable. I had built up a pretty good tolerance since that blackout at the pledge lineup.

When I finally decided to eat those magic mushrooms on the D-Day of my junior year, bumping into Kerry again was the last thing I expected. The day started at Lambda Sigma Delta's annual "Car Smash." Each D-Day, the fraternity got a local junkyard to drag a jalopy onto the school's quadrangle and let kids take a sledgehammer to it for a dollar apiece. If you wanted a second swing, you had to pay twice. Destroying a car must have "paired" well with the psilocybin since many kids took multiple turns. We donated all the money to a local charity so the university allowed us to keep doing it. They were also oblivious to the fact that it catered to the large portion of the student body tripping their faces off.

I was finishing off a 40 ounce bottle of Schlitz when I made the decision to finally indulge. I was standing inside the university post office when Dolf took out his baggie. It felt like a spontaneous call on my part but I must have already made it on some level. Nonetheless, I still wanted to do it before I lost my nerve.

"Dolf, is the rest of that eighth already spoken for?"

"For you, Luca? I didn't think you were into tripping. It would be an honor to give it to you."

"Any last-minute advice?"

"Yeah. They taste real chalky so you'll want to wash it down with my Schlitz."

I didn't know that there was anything in the world that tasted so bad that you'd want to wash it down with malt liquor. The blue and white residue of caps and stems looked more like brain fragments. Maybe that was the Schiltz talking, however. Dolf was right about the taste and I quickly gulped down the malt liquor afterwards. I then naively asked him if he was worried someone would come inside the post office only to see us lapping at the inside of a Glad sandwich bag.

"Come on, Luca. *It's D-Day.*"

As we re-emerged into the sunshine, I was both excited and afraid for whatever would come next. As I wobbled back to the car smash, I spotted Money. I was about to tell him about my decision, but his eyes told me he was already dealing with his own trip.

"HIT . . . THE . . . CAR." The deliberate way in which he spoke those words suggested he was trying to steady himself.

After I slammed the sledgehammer into the defenseless 1985 Volkswagen Dasher, he asked me if I could feel the difference.

"Nah. I don't think they're working. I feel like I've smoked a whole lot of pot, but that's it. Maybe I should eat some more."

"Don't worry," he laughed. "You've eaten enough. Just give it a few minutes."

I stepped back and watched waves of other students finish the job on the Dasher. With twisted grins on their faces, they went after the windshield, the rear-view mirror, even the fucking radio. As each one passed the sledgehammer to the next they flashed a smile to signal that they were in on the "big joke." I wondered if I'd ever join them.

It was somewhere around Alpha Upsilon, on the edge of the quad, when the mushrooms started to take hold. This was nothing like drinking or smoking. My peripheral vision suddenly seemed limitless, as if I could see 360 degrees around myself. It became understandably difficult to stay steady. I saw a couple of familiar faces, but didn't know what to say to them. I'd never had *that* problem before. I looked at one of the rooftops off the quad and spotted a familiar blue baseball hat with stitched gold letters that read "CHARGERS." I thought I was the only person on campus who owned a hat like that.

As my eyes tried to recalibrate themselves, I realized that it *was* my hat. It was on Kerry's head. I had left it in her apartment after the last time we slept together. Even I wasn't selfish enough to try to retrieve it after that. Plus, it looked way better on her at that moment. When she turned around, her brown ponytail swept behind her to reveal those warm blue eyes and I knew I was in serious fucking trouble.

I screamed up to the roof. "Kerry! I need your help!"

She screamed something I couldn't quite make out. Then she tossed her car keys down. As they raced towards me, they left a blurry trail in the air. I panicked for a second but blindly reached my right hand out as they landed smack in the center of my palm.

As I waited for her to come down the stairs to meet me, I wondered what I would say. Before I could figure it out, the words flew out of my mouth:

"I'm tripping on mushrooms and I don't know what to do."

"Oh, honey . . ."

Even with her sympathetic tone, I still wondered if she would turn me away. If she had, I don't how I would have survived the day. The psilocybin was really starting to kick in at this point. Kerry was undoubtedly pissed about the way I'd left things, but it only took one glance into my eyes to know that I was in no shape to defend myself.

"Let's get out of here." She took her car keys from my hand.

As we walked towards her car, I noticed that the fraternity quad looked like a war zone. There were kegs and plastic cups everywhere. Eight different songs were blaring at once from various mounted speakers. Some kids were throwing footballs, baseballs, and Frisbees while others were drinking, screaming, and puking. I wondered how many of them had taken hallucinogens. All I knew is that I wanted to get off campus, fast.

Kerry drove a black Jeep Cherokee and had already taken the hard top off. Since there were no doors on the outside, I spent the entire drive to her apartment frozen in fear that I'd somehow roll out. It was also the first time I'd really seen the city of Rochester during the day. Her apartment and the bar she worked was in a pretty rough part of town. I made sure my seatbelt was fastened and thought that maybe I should be a little more careful where I hung out off-campus.

When we got into her apartment, she asked what I wanted to do first. *First?* The idea of doing even one thing was scary at that point. However, I knew she had tripped before, which explained the calm she was exuding.

"Rob, I have a few old stuffed animals you can play with if you want to."

This was not what I wanted or needed to hear. "I may be a Deadhead, but I'm not a fucking hippie!" That came out way harsher and quicker than I intended. Impulse control was clearly not my strength at that moment.

I suddenly noticed that my fingers felt like they had soda running through them. I tested them out on the corduroy pillows Kerry had scattered on her couch. Every groove registered as I ran my hands across them and she seemed happy I finally found something to focus on.

"Do you want to at least listen to some Dead? You left a tape here the last time you . . ."

Before she could finish her sentence, I told her to put it on.

It was my copy of the second set from 6/15/85, Berkeley. Like my Chargers hat, I forgot I had left it here. Perhaps the universe was punishing me for my cowardice. In the type of justice usually found in *The Twilight Zone*, my favorite band brought me no comfort. I was actually scared shitless. I must have been the only Deadhead in history that didn't enjoying hearing them on psychedelics. Kerry put the tape on mid-set, during "Terrapin Station." The band was whipping itself into a frenzy as they repeated the song's climatic sequence with greater and greater intensity. Once they reached the crescendo, the drummers began their nightly solo. This time, however, the music sounded twisted and dark.

When Kerry asked me why I wanted her to shut it off, I mumbled something about wishing she'd started the tape at the beginning.

She ejected it, but quickly noted that she wasn't buying my explanation.

"That doesn't sound like you at all. What are you thinking about right now?"

I wasn't thinking about anything because I was afraid to focus on any one topic. If I did, I might not be able to get off it. Suddenly, being in her apartment again felt like too much to handle. It wasn't at all like the other times I was here. On those nights, I felt completely comfortable. I hadn't really admitted that to myself before. Was that the reason Kerry and I weren't together?

I lied and told her that I wondered what my parents would do if they knew I was tripping.

"Why don't you call them?" She handed me the phone receiver.

"Call who?"

"Your parents."

"You want me to call my parents? Are you out completely of your mind?"

"Rob, you should go with whatever you're feeling. It's basically the reason people take psychedelics, but you're fighting it. Here, look at these."

She handed me a hardcover book with some impressionist paintings. At least that's what I assumed it was. I didn't know shit about art. Everything was starting to look like there was a strobe light projecting from the back of my head. I had always heard that people didn't get "visuals" on mushrooms. I guess Dolf must have given me some especially good ones. I realized that she was telling me to let go just as Money had after that first suite party. However, this was too intense for me to let go.

"This was a mistake," I mumbled.

"Do you want to go for another drive? We can even go back to *your* room if it would make you feel better."

I had no idea what I wanted to do. There were about a million ideas caroming off the inside of my skull, but the most dominant one was the fear that I would never come down from this trip. The dam was breaking inside my head. I wasn't afraid that I'd actually *do* something crazy, but feared that I couldn't stop myself from doing anything that popped into my head.

That was when I ran into her bathroom and threw up.

Kerry seemed pretty nonplussed. She told me that mushrooms don't agree with a lot of people's stomachs, but that I might have a far mellower trip now that they were out of my system.

"Maybe now you'll stop fighting it. Do you want to smoke some pot? It'll even you out."

"I shouldn't have done this to begin with. More drugs will just make it worse. This is all just bad."

"Why don't you just lie on the couch?"

I was about to joke that this was beginning to feel like therapy, but this was nothing like that. I wasn't quite getting stuck in my anxiety, but I felt like I was hiding from something. Maybe finally lying down wouldn't be such a bad idea.

I put one of those corduroy pillows under my head and

stretched out. I could feel myself instantly melting into the cushions. I didn't realize how exhausted I was until then. I suddenly felt more relaxed than I had all day.

Kerry must have sensed this as she walked over to the couch. "Mind if I lie down?"

I was surprised, but silently scooted back. She lay on her side and wriggled into me. We were spooning pretty closely, but that didn't stop me from trying to move into the warm vacuum between us.

She didn't say anything, but I could feel her body tense up. I felt emotionally closer to her at that moment than I did at any time during sex. I tried to verbalize my epiphany:

"I think I'm getting horny."

"Take a cold shower," she laughed.

Wait. That's not what I meant. Let's try this again.

"I'm very happy right now," I said. She didn't respond. I knew she had some justifiable reservations, but I also knew that she was happy too.

"Kerry, whatever happened with us?"

"You don't have to do this," she coldly stated.

She was right. I shouldn't say it unless I meant it. "No, Kerry. You were right. I'm so into my world of the fraternity, the Chargers, and the Dead that I haven't left room for anything else. I don't know what happened with you and that guy before. But that's not me."

As the words came out of my mouth, I wondered if I could back them up. I was moving into uncharted territory. It was like when I first discovered my "interests." This felt more important, but also threatened to wipe them all out. Then again, maybe the payoff would be worth it.

"Rob, I know you mean those things now, but . . ."

Words weren't going to convince her of the seriousness of my intentions. We just lay in silence for what felt like hours. Eventually, Kerry said she had to go to work.

"Are you going to be okay?"

I told her I would. I was more than okay. When she finally rolled off the futon, breaking the seal between us, I knew things would never be the same. When our relationship finally blossomed, Kerry told me how touched she was that I came to her on D-Day. Although it was seemingly by chance, larger forces seemed to be at work that day.

That was the only time I took mushrooms, but it left me with one very important lesson. When you surrender to a love that powerful, you leave yourself in a very precarious position. However, you have really no choice but to give yourself to that other person; that's what makes it all worthwhile. Robert De Niro essentially said the same thing in the opening scene of *Casino*. Of course, his car was being detonated at the time, but that's not the point.

Kerry and I didn't see each other for a few weeks after that. I think that was because we both knew we had shared something that day, even if we hadn't actually hooked up. The only question was whether either of us was going to do anything about it. As she was set to graduate that May, we were both probably taking that decision even more seriously.

TIME TO SEE WITH BOTH EYES

AS MY JUNIOR YEAR WAS CLOSE to ending, I knew I needed to start thinking about life after college. But at that moment, I was more concerned about what I was going to do about Kerry. It may not have been entirely my fault that we hadn't explored our connection, but it felt like that after D-Day. This could also have been another example of my self-indulgence. I'd still have to be the one to initiate matters, regardless.

Kerry was moving back home to Buffalo after her upcoming graduation until she found a teaching job. Hollywood and I were set to move into an off-campus apartment that summer which we would keep for the following school year. I knew I couldn't let her go back to Buffalo without even giving things a shot.

The University of Rochester distributed diplomas by department after the general ceremony in the football stadium. They grouped students according to major in smaller lecture halls later on to receive their actual degrees. I knew Kerry's entire family would be in the audience at the English department ceremony, so I decided to wait for her in the lobby. It was one thing to finally confront my feelings; I wasn't ready to meet her parents in the same day.

I drove to the nearest 7-11 to buy a bouquet of roses. As I gave my money to the cashier, I wondered if the flowers were more like a peace offering than a romantic gesture. Would Kerry be pissed that I had waited until the day she was set to leave college to step up? It was a chance I had to take. For all of the time I spent inside my own head, I was starting to realize that when it came to the big decisions your true desires and intentions found their way to the forefront.

I threw a collared shirt on top of an old Lambda Sig tee, which passed for formal wear in those days. I got to the lobby just in time to see everyone filing out of the ceremony. When I first spotted Kerry, I froze. As soon her face softened, however, I knew I had made the right decision. As I approached her, I could also tell that she was a little drunk.

I was about to explain my appearance when she grabbed me and gave me a deep kiss on the lips. "*Raaaaahhhhhhhhbbb . . .*" Her usual rasp had a little champagne slur to it that made it even more alluring than usual.

"I'm *so happy* you showed. I was beginning to worry you'd lose your nerve."

Before I could respond, she grabbed my hand and started

leading me towards the crowd. I quickly realized that she was going to introduce me to her family after all. She must have sensed my panic because she passed me a pint of Jameson. I took a quick pull and followed her. There was nothing I could do now.

"Mom, Dad, this is Rob. Remember, he's the boy I told you about?"

Rather than be freaked out by such advance billing, I was touched that she had mentioned me at all. I never thought of her as being romantic about us before. The fact that she referred to me as a "boy" while holding a flask of whiskey was both amusing and endearing.

I worried for a moment that the Jameson would be on my breath, but quickly realized her parents wouldn't care. In fact, she passed the flask to her dad before introducing me. He looked just like the character actor Donald Moffat (the president from *Clear and Present Danger*), but with a more grizzled edge. He couldn't have been more pleasant, however. Her mom was a small, bespectacled schoolteacher with a short mop of salt and pepper hair. She looked docile in comparison to her husband, but their back and forth banter suggested they were a perfect match. I made small talk with both of them for about ten minutes or so before meeting all three of Kerry's siblings. Just like her parents, they all seemed like they came out of central casting for the roles of a large Irish Catholic family. They were actually named Ryan, Sean, and Kaitlyn. They had all previously attended Rochester as well and made me feel very comfortable, all things considered. Who knew what Kerry had told them about us? The fact that I wasn't getting the shit kicked out of me seemed like a positive sign. Just as I started to wonder what all this meant for Kerry and me, her dad announced that they were headed back to Buffalo for a big graduation party at their house.

"Don't worry, Rob. I don't expect you to come with us," she whispered.

Once again, she knew exactly where my head was. *Fuck*. I was a little embarrassed that I was still worried about committing to her after everything that had happened that day.

"It's okay, Rob. You'll get to Buffalo another time." She grabbed my face, gave me a quick whiskey-laden kiss, and began walking away.

She might have known me better than I even knew myself.

"I'll call you at your parents' tonight!"

I couldn't believe how confident I sounded, almost enthusiastic. With an extra spring in my step, I decided to head over to my future digs and hang with Hollywood.

Hollywood's old roommate wouldn't move out for a week, as he had also graduated that day. But he was out celebrating with his family and wouldn't be back until later that night. I sat out on what would soon be my 12th floor balcony, drinking canned Buds and listening to live Springsteen. We got through all three discs of the *Live 1975–85* box set, so I had a nice buzz on by the time I called Kerry in Buffalo. If I was on my way to getting day drunk, she was completely shitfaced. It sounded like she was on truth serum, which was probably what she thought when I had been on mushrooms. No matter what, I felt really good.

"*Raaaaahhhhhhhhhb*, you showed up . . ."

"Yeah, I thought that . . ."

"*Raaaaahhhhhhhhhb* . . ."

"What?"

"I had a feeling about you . . ."

Every time I tried to steer the conversation towards when we would try to get together (and what an actual date might entail), she would hit me with another "*Raaaaahhhhhhhhhb*." Although each one hit its mark and I had a smile throughout, I still wasn't clear on what our next step was. I was set to leave for the Dead's summer tour in a few weeks and needed to find a way to pay for gas and lodging. Yet everything seemed a lot less daunting after talking to Kerry. She ended the conversation by assuring me that *"wuuhhr gonna see each other . . ."* Her tone was almost like that of a little kid teasing her playmate.

We both settled in for our respective summers after her graduation. I locked down a summer job delivering pizza in Rochester's suburbs while Kerry re-acclimated to living with her parents. We made plans to have dinner and she suggested the bar she had worked at before graduation.

"I didn't even know they served food other than wings and waffle fries," I said.

"There's a lot you don't know, Rob."

"What do you mean by that?"

"I mean that we never really got to know each other outside of college."

"But school only ended a couple of weeks ago . . ."

"Just meet me at the bar. Also, Rob?"

"Yeah?"

"Don't expect that I'm going to go home with you."

I discovered a lot more at dinner than just the bar's surprisingly deep menu. It wasn't easy for Kerry growing up. Her dad had suffered a series of heart attacks and her mom's lifetime of smoking had finally caught up with her in the form of emphysema. Her sister Kaitlyn was the "golden child." She was extremely pretty and everything seemed to come effortlessly for her. Ryan and Sean might have taught her how to appreciate booze and football, but she found it tough to relate to them on a deeper level.

True to her word, she drove back to Buffalo after dinner. Before she did, however, she kissed me in a way that I told me we'd see each other again before too long.

That year's summer tour would have me on the road for nine days while traveling through New York, New Jersey, and Ohio. My pizza job would not only help finance the trip but also gave me the flexibility to take the time off. But would being away fuck up things with Kerry? Before I could begin to worry, she surprised me yet again with an idea.

"Why don't I come with you to the Washington show at the end of June?"

We still hadn't discussed the few Dead shows she had seen since high school. I had certainly never considered sharing that part of my life with her. My plans were to meet some fellow Delts at RFK Stadium in DC before driving back to Rochester the following day. The infinite energy of a 21-year-old allowed me to perform such feats back then. I told Kerry that I hadn't even booked a hotel in Washington yet.

"That's okay. We can always get a room together if things go well."

I knew this was an opportunity I couldn't miss. Even though it took me out of my way, I picked her up at her parents' house in Buffalo. We pulled onto the New York State Thruway in my parents' 1986 Isuzu Trooper and settled in for the long drive.

"What tapes do you have the besides the Dead? I think you'll hear more than enough of that this weekend."

"There's a case under your seat," I told her.

"Creedence, Warren Zevon, Dylan . . . I had no idea you listened to anything *but* the Dead."

"Thanks, I guess."

"*Springsteen, Boston 5-31-78*? I love Bruce! I saw him at the Buffalo War Memorial in high school."

"I'm impressed."

"I fell down the stairs in the middle of the show. I still have the scar on my leg. It didn't stop me from enjoying the best show of my life."

"Now I'm more than impressed," I said. "I think I might be a little turned on."

"Pace yourself, Rob. It's a long trip."

The best part of the drive was when we weren't saying anything at all. With Springsteen blasting, we just enjoyed the each other's company without conversation. About two hours outside of Washington, she pulled my Chargers hat from out of her purse and popped a new tape in the deck. I immediately recognized the opening notes of "China Cat Sunflower" from the Greek Theatre set I'd last heard on Dandelion Day. It had been only two months, but felt like years ago. As we flew down the Beltway with the evening air coming through the open windows, the music wasn't the only thing that seemed a lot less scary since then and not just because she had rewound the tape to the beginning.

I was just about to suggest that we start thinking about finding a room when Kerry said we should check out some of the sights.

"Come on, Rob. I've never been to the National Mall. *I'll make it fun . . .*"

She had that alluring tone to her voice that she knew I couldn't say no to. Before I knew it, we had parked the car and were walking towards the Capitol building. It was a beautiful June night and all the monuments were softly glowing. As we sat on the steps in front of the rotunda, it felt like we were all alone.

Kerry put her hand on my thigh and told me to relax. Before I knew what was happening she was going down on me.

"Woah . . ."

I should have been worried that someone spotted us, but it felt way too good for anything else to creep into my brain. I'm sure Hunter Thompson would have made some perverse connection to the American Dream, but all I could do was just lay back on the steps in awe. I looked up at the full moon, but it was too bright to look at. I closed my eyes and dug my fingers into her brown hair as I felt my face break into a massive smile.

When it was over, Kerry looked up with a mischievous grin.

"Feeling patriotic, Rob?"

"Uh, maybe we should find that hotel now."

After having sex for the first time since the fall, we both fell asleep instantly. The next morning I woke up even earlier than usual for a show. I let Kerry sleep and walked to the nearby package store to stock up for the parking lot. As we closed the door to the motel room to begin the drive to the stadium, I looked over at her.

"Have fun last night?"

Before I could respond, she started giggling. This time, I was in on the joke.

We were supposed to meet my friends an hour before show time at the Will Call window. RFK Stadium wasn't in the best part of DC, so we decided to get to the lot before it got too dark. We found a parking spot near a clean patch of grass where we could lay down a blanket. Across the street, we could see the "locals" trying to entice concertgoers to park in their driveway. They were drinking what looked like a bottle of Everclear vodka and were getting more and more impatient with each rejection. Before too long, they were pounding the hoods of approaching cars. Kerry and I just sat on the blanket laughing our asses off. We had cold beers to drink and the tape deck had auto-reversed into the second half of the Greek show. We weren't due to meet my friends for a bit, so I was at complete ease.

The show was great that night and the band dusted off "Casey Jones" for the first time in eight years. As soon as they started with "Drivin' that train," the crowd went berserk. During the ensuing bedlam, I sneaked a look at look over at Kerry. Her smile revealed that she knew how special the moment was. Her understanding and being there to share it with me made it that much more special. Whatever I was feeling, I knew I didn't want it to go away.

For the rest of that summer, Kerry and I were able to keep the blissfulness going. I figured things would be the same once I started my senior year. I had no idea what I would do after my graduation, but everything in my life seemed set up perfectly. But once again I would soon see how much there was that I didn't know.

KINDA FRIGHTENING

ALONG WITH MY SENIOR YEAR, fall brought the annual beginning of football season. Even with all the Dead shows and Delt parties, I still made sure to watch the Chargers every Sunday. Back then you needed a satellite dish to watch any out of market NFL games and the only place to see a team as unpopular as the Chargers was to find a place that showed *all* the games. When on tour, that meant I needed to find a sports bar that fit the bill.

Fortunately, there was such a place right near school when I was on campus. The Bolts finished in last place during both of my first two years in college. My junior year they finished 4-12 and I even got my fake ID confiscated on the last day of the season. I was able to find a new one shortly thereafter, but they began the next season by losing their first four games. No team had ever made the playoffs after a start like that, so it seemed inevitable they'd miss the postseason for a *tenth* consecutive year.

I had no choice but to miss the next game since it was Yom Kippur, the holiest of Jewish holidays. I would be back in Chappaqua, and my parents had plans to have my relatives over. Since the Chargers had just lost 27-0 the previous week, I didn't think I'd be missing much. But after dinner, I couldn't help but sneak away to call "Sports Phone," the 900 number that gave you all the scores in the pre-internet age.

I anxiously waited as the recorded voice read the scores of that day's action. Since you were billed by the second, they weren't exactly rushing through the message. Of course, the Chargers were the last score given.

"San Diego Chargers 17, Seattle Seahawks 6."

I didn't expect them to win and for a second wondered if my not watching had helped. They were off with a bye the following week so I had time to ponder that question.

I had mostly experienced the Chargers through television. I saw them when they visited the Jets or Giants, but was otherwise relegated to waiting for a score update during one of *those* teams' games. They didn't even have the scores scrolling on the bottom of the screen back then; you'd only get an update when something big happened. Now I could watch them for myself at a bar and they were awful. This week was the exception, apparently.

The next Sunday after the bye week, I decided to stay home from the bar. It couldn't do any harm, right? The Chargers beat the Colts by 20 points. Two more weeks went by of me staying home and they kept winning. They then beat the Colts a second time 26-0, had a .500 record, and had as many wins as they had the season before. Next up was a game at the first-place Kansas City Chiefs. Shit was getting serious.

When I didn't get to sleep until 5:00 AM the night after a Delt party, it seemed like the decision as to whether I should watch at the bar had been already made for me. I rolled over at 12:30 PM, and decided I would just watch the local game and wait for updates. The Bills were playing the Steelers.

Kerry was actually at the game with her brothers. She hadn't come to visit that weekend in order to start tailgating early. At least that's what I told myself. In reality, things were beginning to cool off since the Dead show in DC. It was more than the end of our "honeymoon period." We were only an hour away from each other, but seemingly in two entirely different places. She was still living at home while she waited for a teaching job to open up in Buffalo. Compared to me, she was living in the real world.

I knew things were different between us after the first time she visited that fall. We were sitting in the living room eating bagels when I noticed the change. Throughout the summer, we'd shared a bunch of breakfasts in the very same room. In fact, we'd had sex a few times on that couch when Hollywood stayed out. Suddenly things felt tense for no apparent reason as I struggled to make small talk.

"How's the teaching search going?"

She looked pissed that I even asked.

"It's hard, Rob. Every girl with an English degree wants to be a teacher. I've been close to a few jobs, but no offers."

"Yeah, I can understand. That's gotta suck."

"How could you understand? You're in your senior year of college."

That seemed uncalled for. She was in my situation a year ago. I decided to ignore her slight in the hopes of getting through breakfast. After a few more barbs during future awkward meals, however, it was clear things were deteriorating between us.

That was just one of many things I didn't want to face that fall. For one, I still had no idea what I would do after graduation. The only career path that made sense at all with a history degree was law school. If I could get into SUNY Buffalo, Kerry and I could even get a place together. Even though we never discussed the possibility, I was grasping at straws in my own head. I was looking for any solution that would keep us together. Just like with everything else, I dug in more the worse things got. However, I was clearly overcompensating for a relationship that was dying of natural causes. I even took an LSAT prep course that summer. Sitting in a cubicle at the nearest Stanley Kaplan, I started to wonder what the hell I had gotten myself into.

The morning of the Kansas City game, I was at least focused only on football. It kept my other worries away, at least for a while. Through the updates provided by NBC during the Bills game, I saw that the Chargers were behind 13-0 in the first half. I was disappointed, but finally had enough energy to roll off my futon and go out into the living room. As I entered the living room, I saw Hollywood having some beers with another brother of ours, DJ. I popped one open and sat down to watch the second half.

Through the updates on the bottom of the screen, I saw that the Chargers were coming back. As the Bills officially put the Steelers away, the Bolts scored their second touchdown and took a one-point lead late in the 4th quarter. The announcers then revealed that the network was going to provide its viewers with "bonus coverage of the nail-biter in Kansas City." I was going to have to make a decision about watching the game after all. I had made all this effort not to, but it seemed like the universe wanted me to tune in. That had to mean *something*, right?

DJ, normally a man of few words, warned me about the consequences.

"Luca, man, you don't fuck with mojo."

"But what's the point of them winning if I can't see it? I shouldn't be denied that, Deej."

I moved back on the couch to see if the Chargers defense could hold. Of course, the Chiefs put together a final drive and kicked the winning field goal as time ran out.

"Luca, I don't mean to say I told you so . . ."

"Gee thanks, DJ. I'm glad you don't *mean* to say it even as you currently are."

That's when the idea hit me. In the spirit of *Animal House*, I needed another stupid and futile gesture if I wanted to turn things around.

The Chargers would be in Cleveland the following week, only a few hundred miles outside of Buffalo. There was only one way to make things right. I picked up the phone and asked the operator for the number for Ticketmaster.

"You want Chicken Master, sir?"

I told her no, but thought I should file that other option away in the back of my mind. There weren't too many chicken places that delivered downtown.

SUNDAY MORNING, WHIP COMING DOWN

AFTER TAKING THE LSAT IN AUGUST, I knew the scores would be arriving any day. I felt like I had done okay, but probably not well enough to get me into SUNY Buffalo, a highly competitive school. When they came the day before the Chargers game in Cleveland, I wasn't completely surprised that they were pretty average. I hadn't considered any other schools because I really wasn't that committed to going to begin with. There were many levels of denial inside my head at that moment. Kerry and I had plans to meet for breakfast on my way to the game Sunday morning. This seemed like the kind of thing I should tell her in person, but I sure wasn't looking forward to it.

To make things worse, I woke up to the early stages of a major snowstorm that Sunday. Given our location, I shouldn't have been that surprised, but back then I didn't think about things like checking the weather conditions.

By the time we finally hit Buffalo, DJ was still asleep in the passenger seat of the Subaru. I had swapped the Trooper with my parents before the year started and was starting to really regret it. The GL Wagon had four-wheel drive at least. When I pulled into the parking lot, I told DJ I was meeting Kerry. He just mumbled that I should leave the car's heat on. I cracked the window a little and left him in there to sleep. I didn't want him spontaneously exploding like some Spinal Tap drummer. As soon as I saw Kerry, I felt that all-too-familiar tension begin to rise. I sat down at the booth across from her and noticed that she looked pretty tense. This wasn't good. Maybe we just needed to say it to each other. We were drifting apart and my not staying in Western New York after graduation would just expedite things. In the end, that might be for the best.

After we both made small talk over coffee and eggs, I delivered my news.

"My LSAT scores came back yesterday."

"How'd you do?"

"Pretty good . . ."

"What does 'pretty good' mean?"

"Not good enough to get into SUNY Buffalo."

"Oh," she paused. Then she asked the inevitable question: "Are you all right?"

"Actually, I am. I don't think I ever saw myself as a lawyer. I have no idea what I'm going to do after graduation next year except catch some Dead shows before real life starts."

I was being truthful, but was also more disappointed than I was letting on. I really, really, needed the Chargers to win that day.

By the time I got back to the car, the snow was really starting to come down. We had to take the New York State Thruway to its very end before moving into Pennsylvania and then Ohio. I needed to pick up the pace. When I put my key in the ignition, DJ started snoring loudly, seemingly as a response to the revving from the engine.

The farther I drove, the less the roads seemed to be plowed. Of course, the snow was picking up, which might have had something to do with it. It seemed like I was driving right into the teeth of the storm. By the time we reached Pennsylvania, the thruway was entirely covered. Maybe I wasn't even meant to be at this game. Maybe DJ was right. Was I fucking with the team's mojo while completely putting my life in jeopardy? That's when I saw a snowcat pull out about fifty feet ahead.

Suddenly, there was hope. I popped a Dead tape in the deck in celebration. It was the FM simulcast of my third show— Saratoga Springs, 6/28/88. The tape was in heavy rotation for me at the time, so I had left it in the middle of the first set at "Row Jimmy." Jerry sang about a broken heart not being so bad when you didn't have what you mistakenly thought you did. While possibly poignant, these weren't words I wanted to hear. I needed a soundtrack to take things to the next level, so I grabbed an unmarked cassette and threw it in the deck.

It was the only unlabeled tape in my collection, so I knew it had to be my only hip-hop entry. Each side had one of the two big debuts of the year, House of Pain and Cypress Hill. I was hoping for the latter because they struck me as a little more authentic. Fortunately, I got my wish as the first song kicked in. As the nasal twang of B-Real rapped about how he could just kill a man, DJ finally woke up.

The snowcat was leaving a perfect trail for me to drive behind, but it wouldn't stay clear for long. I had to make sure I didn't miss my chance. When I saw a car attempting to merge onto the interstate in front of me, I quickly accelerated. Even in 4-wheel drive, the car fishtailed. After regaining control, I felt a huge sense of relief. DJ, who was now fully awake, clearly didn't share it.

"Luca, what the fuck are you doing?"

"Don't worry, Deej. I think we'll still make it by kickoff."

"Are you out of your mind? I don't care about the game. You're gonna get us killed!"

"How, exactly?"

"Pull the car over and I'll drive."

It took about five minutes for me to surrender control of the wheel. If I hadn't seen the snowcat exit off the road, I don't know if I would have even done it willingly. But I also needed a release after over two hours of intensely focused driving and there was a 12 pack of Rolling Rock cans in the backseat. It was 45 minutes to kickoff and the last sign I saw said we were about 40 miles outside of Cleveland. There was nothing left for me to do. Cypress Hill and Rolling Rock seemed like a good combination.

The subsequent buzz made me simultaneously a little *less* worried that we'd be late to the game and a little *more* fired up when we got into the lot just after 1:00 PM. As we began running from the car to the gate, I heard a huge cheer from the hometown crowd. The Chargers had already thrown an interception, apparently. Once we reached our seats, however, things started looking up. Stan Humphries threw a 26-yard touchdown pass to put the Bolts ahead.

Humphries was a castoff from the Redskins who'd only become the starting quarterback after the guy ahead of him went down with a season-ending injury. He was a chunky guy with a pug nose. But he had a big arm and even bigger balls. His gunslinger mentality also caused eight interceptions in those first four losses before he started to turn things around.

The Browns countered with 13 unanswered points. The snow was lightening up and the crowd was starting to get pretty loud. Cleveland Stadium was no place to be rooting for the visiting team in those days. The team was tough, as were its fans. The ones in the "Dawg Pound" in the east end zone once snuck an entire keg into the stadium and would shower the other team with dog biscuits, eggs, and even batteries. However, they couldn't detect my allegiance that day beyond my faded Chargers ski hat. I simply sat in my frozen plastic seat mumbling to myself and DJ that this was too big a game to lose.

Late in the fourth quarter, the Chargers had the ball in Cleveland territory. Humphries spotted All-Pro wide receiver Anthony Miller in the end zone. He hurled the ball 45 yards only to see it sail barely over Miller's fingertips. But true to form, Humphries went right back to him on the next play with the exact same call. This time, Miller caught it for a touchdown and the stadium fell silent. Maybe I couldn't fuck up their chances by witnessing it firsthand.

When the Chargers sealed the win with a fumble recovery, I knew the fans would be looking for a scapegoat. DJ and I grabbed a discarded bedsheet banner and held it over our heads just as the first torrent of snowballs came down. We started running towards the car and got back reasonably unscathed. When looked at the banner during our getaway, we saw that it read "SANDUSKY

LOVES THE BROWNS." It was too good to throw away, so we put it up in the fraternity's lounge that night.

We drank the rest of the Rolling Rock and admired our souvenir. Stan Humphries and the Chargers won the rest of their games that season and are still the only team to make the playoffs after a 0-4 start. But that night, I was just happy that my watching them hadn't derailed the season. Plus, it was nice not to think about things with Kerry for a few hours. I'd need that more and more during my senior year.

WANDER 'ROUND

WHILE LAMBDA SIGMA DELTA never thought of itself as belonging to anything, it was really just a single chapter of an Indiana-based national fraternity. We viewed national like an annoying parent that was too far away to know what we were up to and too stupid to understand it. They owned the three Greek letters that made us a legitimate organization, but as long as they got a share of our membership dues we assumed they'd leave us alone. What we didn't consider was that in exchange for licensing their brand, they had to insure us. The words "risk management" would soon be all too familiar.

We had little in common with other nearby chapters of LSD, but the chapter at SUNY Brockport sounded like they were from an entirely different planet even though they were less than thirty minutes away. Brockport wasn't the academic institution Rochester was, which meant that drinking was way more out in the open. From what I had heard, the campus was full of white, Western New York types who loved to party, and the LSDs were their kings. As their brothers, we were welcome to pop in at any time.

Kerry and I still spoke on the phone at this point, but after that morning in the diner, things were never the same. It wasn't my inability to get into SUNY Buffalo that seemed to upset her, as much as the fact I had absolutely no plan for post-graduation life. At least that's what I'd get from our increasingly less frequent phone conversations:

"What are you going to do next year? You can't just hang out with your fraternity brothers for the rest of your life."

I quoted Boon from *Animal House* and said, "When I graduate, I'm gonna get drunk every night."

"I get the reference, Rob, but I don't think you're completely joking. You're not ready to put effort into anything, except preserving your life right now. We won't have any kind of relationship after graduation unless we work at it."

Five months earlier, we were in love with each other and it never occurred to me that we'd be apart. Now that things weren't coming so easy for us, I knew that we were in trouble. Our not being in the same place made it that much easier to abandon the relationship. I didn't understand why something that made me feel so good now required effort to sustain.

"You're one year out of college and you suddenly have all the answers? You're living at home and substitute teaching. It's not like you're so much better than me."

To her credit, Kerry kept her cool.

"Rob, I think we shouldn't talk for a while. I'm about to say a lot of things I know I'll regret."

I needed another distraction and figured this was a good time to visit our Brockport brethren. I decided to turn it into a pledge activity and make it an event. Since becoming a brother, I had gone pretty easy on the incoming Delts-in-training. After bringing it up one night in the lounge, Dolf explained why the older brothers weren't interested in coming along.

"We took a trip to Brockport years ago. It was fun, but kinda got old. You'll see what I mean."

This sounded like the warning Charlton Heston gets in *Planet of the Apes* before he goes down the beach to see the Statue of Liberty. "You may not like what you find," in the words of Dr. Zaius. I wasn't worried I'd find out some deep secret about the human experience. If anything, it made me more curious what Dolf was talking about.

DJ and I put together a crew we thought would be up to the task. Chilly Willy was a squat Chinese stoner from New Jersey. He had the face and build of "Oddjob" from *Goldfinger* mixed with the oily shoulder-length hair of every kid who went dirtbag in the suburbs. "H.W." was an All-American type from Texas, thus the Bush-inspired nickname. For a while, we all wondered if he even knew what fraternity he was pledging. After talking with him one night after a lineup, however, it became clear he loved our outlaw vibe. Of course, it took several hits of acid for his views on authority and personal freedom to come out.

To keep an eye on the pledges (since we couldn't be bothered to do it), we enlisted the most responsible brother we knew. "Good Guy" was not only his nickname but a perfect description of his personality. He was a studious-looking Jewish kid from Westport, Connecticut who majored in psychology. Good Guy was always the most levelheaded among us, even though that wasn't saying much. He acted as our conscience by reminding us of the unintended consequences of whatever stupid thing we were about to do. Even if we didn't usually listen to his warnings, he was still a lot of fun to hang out with. I always thought he was what I would have ended up like if I listened to everything my parents told me and had never discovered the Grateful Dead.

Since we figured we needed a little muscle in case things got out of hand, we also grabbed Bam Bam. He was a former football player from one of those elite Massachusetts prep schools. His nickname was also spot-on. He liked to break stuff and would often put on the *Conan the Barbarian* soundtrack in the middle of parties when he was about to do it. Somehow, it didn't seem unusual at the time.

The five of us piled into Chilly's brand-new Ford F-150 truck. His dad was apparently a successful surgeon and had given his son an unlimited allowance for college. This was even more evident when he passed back a joint of some of the strongest weed I'd ever smoked. It seemed to knock everyone on their ass, especially Good Guy. Once we were about fifteen minutes from campus, I yelled to Chilly to put on some music. He was still a pledge, after all. He told me that the only tape he kept in the car was the soundtrack to *Aladdin* that the dealership threw in with it.

"Wait, you mean it came with the car? That's like not changing the photo in your wallet after buying it."

"I'm telling you, Luca. *Aladdin*'s actually not half bad."

I told him to pull over so I could get us some 40-ouncers for the party. DJ sprinted alongside me towards the 7-11 after we parked. We decided each guy should get two apiece, but never anticipated how we'd get ten large bottles of malt liquor out of the store. Chilly's potent weed wasn't exactly making either of us too detail-oriented. The guy behind the counter told us he'd need to grab a couple of boxes from the back. That's when I spotted the "HELP WANTED" sign over the cigarettes.

"DJ, I gotta do it."

I could tell by the look on his face that we were both thinking the same thing.

As the clerk was boxing up our malt liquor, I asked him for a job application.

"Deej, what's Good Guy's phone number?"

I didn't have anything good to put for his prior experience, but I made sure to specify that he would only be available to work on weekends. As I was about to pass the finished application over the counter, it hit me. This would be my masterstroke, or so my weed-addled mind thought.

I added "also available to work all Jewish holidays" to the bottom of the page.

DJ, who was looking over my shoulder, started snickering. He couldn't contain himself as we walked out the door with the boxes in hand and broke into full laughter.

"I think it actually makes him stand out as an applicant," I added.

We were able to put on straight faces before getting back into the truck. We were only about ten minutes away, which was just enough time to fortify ourselves with the malt liquor. We hadn't told the Brockport Delts that we were showing up, but they'd issued us a standing invitation in the past. Their pig roast was apparently the biggest party of year, their version of the one-piece party.

We hadn't even reached campus before we started seeing the massive line of cars. They were all surrounding a huge white house with techno music blasting. There seemed to be a hundred students stretched around the block. Chilly pulled over and parked at the nearest corner. He actually parked *on* the corner, as we could feel the curb under the tires.

We grabbed the remaining 40s out of the box and started towards the house. As we got closer, we were awestruck at how many people there were. The University of Rochester couldn't get this many kids to come out for anything. The school was so fragmented by political correctness at that point that even the most popular fraternity couldn't attract a crowd like this.

The brother at the door was holding a sleeve of red Solo cups in in one hand and a cashbox in the other.

"We're from the U of R chapter," I explained.

This All-American meathead looked me over for a moment in skepticism.

"Okay . . . what's the handshake?"

It was a good thing that I was the one to make the introductions because I don't think anyone else in our group could have pulled it off. We only showed pledges the handshake at the end of Hell Week and never used it at meetings even though we were supposed to. Looking at Bam Bam, Good Guy, H.W., Chilly, and DJ, this human tree trunk still wasn't convinced we were brothers.

My affinity to recall minutiae like the handshake, no matter my condition, left him no choice but to let us in.

He gave us each a cup without charging us. Brotherhood had its privileges, clearly. We poured the malt liquor in them and entered the house. We walked through the dining room and towards the music. They had a giant backyard with a full DJ booth set up in the back. There were people dancing around the pig that was slowly rotating on a spit. "House" music definitely wasn't my thing, but the crowd was clearly into this Dionysian ritual. It was no Car Smash, but I could at least understand the appeal.

"Okay, guys. Let's check this place out," I declared.

I told everyone we should use the pig as a meeting place if we got separated. There were at least twice as many people here as at one of our parties. Bam Bam and I decided to venture inside the house. We left the other four and went back through the dining room.

The first thing we noticed was that they used it as an actual dining room. The walls featured composite pictures that went back to the 1930s. Alumni donations probably funded the chandelier, high-backed chairs, and long wooden table. As we looked up the carpeted staircase, there were countless girls coming our way. I spotted a cute pair and was about to ask them about our Brockport brothers when I heard a scream from outside. We'd only been gone ten minutes. How much trouble could those guys have gotten into?

We emerged from the dining room just in time to see H.W. lifting the pig off the spit. I screamed at him to stop, but it was useless. Before I knew it, he was bringing down the carcass onto Chilly's head. He hit him pretty hard, as the pig's head snapped right off. The crowd around the fire looked too shocked to be angry, but I knew that would change shortly. I was about to ask Bam Bam where Good Guy was and why he didn't stop it when I spotted our collective conscience in the sound booth. Deee-Lite's "Groove is in the Heart" quickly dissolved into *Conan*. Before I could even ask him how he got back there, I heard DJ's famous "deep throated growl." That was his battle cry and a sign that things were about to get even weirder. I couldn't figure out where it was coming from, as there was no sign of him in the backyard. That's when I heard someone yell that there was a guy standing outside one of the upstairs windows.

I turned to Bam Bam. "What the fuck?"

"DJ asked to borrow the tape," he said sheepishly.

DJ was now perched outside with his steel-tipped cowboy boots hanging over the ledge.

"Is that guy with you?" It was one of the Brockport brothers screaming over my shoulder. Before I could answer, five more of them started running for the open space beneath the window. They started screaming for DJ to get down. I looked up at him and saw a grin slowly creep across his face.

Shit.

He jumped with his right leg completely extended. The silver toe of his boot was guiding his descent like some drunken superhero. The Brockport brothers were so quick that Bam Bam and I were still lagging behind when DJ landed on them. As the circle broke apart after impact, I could hear one of them screaming in pain.

"He fuckin' cut me!" I could see him holding his cheek where the boot hit him. There was blood streaming from under his hand. DJ, meanwhile, was dusting himself off, and preparing to refill his Solo cup at one of the nearby kegs. His latest victim shut that down immediately.

"You guys are not welcome here. *Leave. Now.*"

I had to admit we weren't being good guests, but it wasn't like we spoiled the Garden of Eden. However, things were only going to get worse if we stuck around. I saw Chilly wiping barbecue sauce off his shoulders and screamed to him.

"Where's Good Guy?"

He had emerged from behind the DJ booth, holding the *Conan* tape. Without giving him a signal, he started running towards the house. We all followed suit and as I caught up to him I noticed something shining from his left ear.

"Dude, did you get an earring?"

"I met this girl by the DJ booth who wanted to pierce it. She liked that I had never gotten one and wanted to be the one to do it. Of course, she had her hand down my pants at the time."

When we got inside the car, I had to find out more details.

"You didn't think it was weird that she had the piercing kit *with her*?"

"I didn't think about that. After DJ's jump, I'm just happy we're never coming back here again."

"Actually," I replied. "How do you feel about commuting to work?"

DJ, who was sitting behind me in the truck, burst out laughing again.

CAN'T TAKE IT WITH YOU

ONE OF THE THINGS that made the Brockport trip so great was the sad truth that we couldn't have those kinds of adventures at our own school anymore. The University of Rochester became successively more restrictive each year I attended. Lambda Sigma Delta was especially ill-suited to deal with this new era of political correctness, where the appearance of an infraction could be more damaging than actually doing something wrong.

Without realizing it, we were being replaced by another fraternity that was simply a sanitized version of us. Pi Phi was established during my freshman year of 1989 and adapted to the changing times infinitely better than we did. In essence, they conformed. Their brothers ran for seats on school government, were visible in campus charities, and even worked *with* the administration. Now they were poaching a lot of the pledges who'd normally join up with us. If the national fraternity functioned as a big insurance agency, our diminishing numbers made us a much less attractive risk to have on the books. Telling them to go fuck themselves at every turn probably wasn't helping.

Every time they sent a risk management representative to visit, it was as if we were daring them to revoke our charter. We dragged one to Canada for a pledge trip that ended up at a strip club. Another walked in on a bong hit that spanned an entire hallway. We were just as resistant with university administration in their numerous attempts to get us to "play ball." I saw this all up close once I became Vice President during my senior year.

It was a warm spring night and the rest of the executive board of the fraternity was on the balcony with me trying to brainstorm new recruitment strategies. We all sat on the long sofa, which had somehow survived another Rochester winter. It looked like the torn orange couch the Pit Boys sat on in *The Wire*. Hollywood was the first to speak.

"What do you want, Luca? Do you want us to become fuckin' Pi Phis?"

Before I could respond, I heard a giant explosion to my right. DJ had thrown his empty 40 ounce bottle at the streetlight in front of the balcony. The sound of a glass-on-glass collision was just the kind of thing that was going to get us run out of town. I quickly turned around.

"I don't want us to sell out, but I just don't want us to die off! The university seems determined to make that happen. Why should we help them?"

As if to answer my question, Money hurled his 40 over my head and knocked out the other light. That's when he and DJ grabbed the couch at both ends, while Hollywood pulled out a lighter.

I had no idea what the couch was made of, but it caught fire pretty quickly. When it hit the asphalt, it kept burning. I knew campus security would be there shortly and that I'd be the one who had to deal with them. As I stood there looking at the fire, I realized that there was no way we could keep the fraternity going. Maybe those guys were right. Had I learned the wrong lesson from *Animal House*? If they're going to nail you no matter what you do, shouldn't you at least have a good time?

The inevitable can still feel shocking, even after you've thrown a burning couch off a balcony. When the university summoned the entire brotherhood to a meeting that spring, I still didn't think they were going to pull the plug. As soon as we entered the conference room, however, campus security appeared at every doorway. Only Hollywood seemed to know what was going on.

"Dude, they're gonna shut us down. I'm going back for the composites."

The annual composite photos of the entire brotherhood hung on the walls of the party room and served as the only true document of the chapter's history. They were what girls checked out during parties and what prospective pledges stared at during rush. They were one of the few conventions we shared with every other fraternity. I had no idea why the national organization would want them even if it *was* the end. Nonetheless, Hollywood darted out the door before security locked the rest of us in.

What followed is still a blur. I'm not sure what the official explanation was for the revocation of our charter. The Dean of Students said only one other fraternity had been kicked off campus in recent memory, but that was for an alleged *gang rape*. I was about to mention the insanity of that point, when I saw the last representative who visited us in the back of the room. I knew then that the decision was already final. He didn't mention the Canadian strip club or ten-foot bong, but addressed our "dwindling membership numbers and our unwillingness to be good citizens on campus." He mentioned that other national reps were at that very moment on their way to our floor to seize both the composite pictures and the wooden letters, which were now stolen property. Hollywood was right.

Luckily by that time, he had already scaled the outside walls and got in through the balcony. In the end, the composites didn't matter. We were officially unrecognized in the eyes of both the national fraternity and the university. We wanted to be outlaws, not total outcasts. The brothers living on the floor were to be relocated by semester's end. Hollywood and I were still living in our apartment, so at least we didn't need to move. I never did find where he hid those composites, however.

"For your own good, you shouldn't know," he once explained.

Sure, we tried to keep it going. We had parties at our new off-campus house and attracted a handful of pledges. We talked about making a triumphant return to glory, but we were already doomed. I was discovering that some things aren't meant to last. What makes them great is what also causes them to destroy themselves.

Our final party at the new off-campus house proved to be a sad but fitting end. Everyone was drinking and listening to music, but it felt like we were all just going through the motions. At least my pledge class was able to experience the fraternity at its peak only a few years earlier. The younger brothers had only heard the stories of greatness. Bam Bam really personified this frustration. He was living at the house and was trying, to no avail, to get the final party going. He was circulating through the crowd and soliciting song requests. When the resulting Public Enemy failed to do the job, he stormed up to his room. I figured that was his last attempt to salvage matters, but he suddenly came down the stairs holding his 1980s Macintosh computer. When he climbed on top of the bar with it under his arm, I knew what he had in mind. Before he could balance himself up to hurl it against the wall, the plywood gave way and he fell through the bar. We all laughed, but like the party itself, it felt hollow. We couldn't even break shit effectively anymore.

The writing was on the wall, or at least shards of plywood. We decided to use our annual spring formal as a final sendoff to LSD. It would be like a Viking Funeral, or an Irish Wake, depending on how it went. We reached out to every alumnus we could and begged them to come back to Rochester for one last weekend. We went ahead and booked a fancy club off-campus that required us to commit financially to a ton of guests. After we sent out the invites to fill that quota, national wrote us a "cease-and-desist" letter since we were using *their* letters and crest. At this point, I finally joined the "fuck it" movement. If it wasn't worth it for them to insure us anymore, it sure as shit wouldn't be in their financial interests to sue us. I even overruled Good Guy, assigned the unenviable task of co-chairing the event with me.

After miraculously getting enough people to commit, I then had to assure the club that we would somehow behave ourselves. I knew there was no way that would happen, but gave my word anyway. I was through worrying about the consequences. It hadn't kept the fraternity going, anyway. I even invited Kerry to be my date. I knew it would be the last time we'd probably see each other, but decided it didn't matter. I was saying "fuck it" across the board. College was ending and everything that made it great appeared to be ending with it. I should at least enjoy it while I could.

The resulting party began with House of Pain's "Jump Around" blaring over the PA. The cover band we hired for the occasion came out and began seamlessly jamming along. I don't know how they found the space for guitars in that song, but they landed in a perfect version of the Allmans' "In Memory of Elizabeth Reed." As I started to lose myself in the music, the club's event manager whispered in my ear.

"Some of your party guests are smoking marijuana in the restroom."

I told her I would take care of it.

Of course, I did no such thing and enjoyed the music from the bar in the back of the ballroom. She returned a few minutes later with a little more urgency to relay that there was a couple "fornicating in the stall." By the time she came back shortly thereafter to tell me that some of the older brothers had broken the bathroom mirror and were snorting lines off it, the party was already ending.

For my efforts in putting the formal together, I was named "Brother of the Year" that night. My reward was a cheap bottle of Pepé Lopez silver tequila. As I got up to give my speech, I realized that this was truly the end of the road for many things. I took a pull off the bottle and tried to put a positive spin on everything, but it felt too weird. I returned to my seat and tried to explain it all to Kerry.

"I'm getting an award from an organization that soon won't exist. How fucked up is that?"

She didn't answer, but instead gave a sympathetic smirk. It wasn't the state of the fraternity that was on her mind. By this time, Hollywood and I had decided to move into an apartment in Manhattan. That was more out of convenience, however, rather than a post-graduation plan. DJ and Money were also moving there. The illusion that we could keep the fraternity going was almost gone but I thought we could all have one last ride together. Inviting Kerry was the same type of futile gesture. Looking at her, I could tell she knew it too.

I took another hit off the Pepé Lopez and my face instantly contorted. Was this the shit I'd been drinking the last four years? It was like a four-year buzz was dissipating and I didn't like what I was feeling. I looked at Kerry and repeated the question, but it sounded more like pleading.

"Seriously, how fucked up is that?"

She just gave a taut smile and softly uttered, "Pretty fucked up."

Maybe closure tastes like cheap tequila, though Tom Cruise's "Brian Flanagan" said it best in *Cocktail*. Everything ends badly.

PART II

Better to Search Since You Can't Stand Still

SING FOR YOUR SUBWAY FARE

WITHIN A FEW MONTHS OF GRADUATION, Hollywood and I found an apartment on the Upper East Side of Manhattan. I found the only job my history degree seemed to qualify me for, a paralegal at a midtown law firm. This was my first full-time job and I suddenly found myself riding the 6 train every morning with a subway full of business types reading their newspapers. The firm was housed in the same building as Citibank, their primary client. As I emerged from the train, I'd look up at that glass and concrete tower before heading for the elevator. I wasn't in college any more, that was for sure. My title might have read "Corporate Legal Assistant," but I was basically a glorified copy boy. Most days I sat inside a burlap-lined cubicle filing documents for the "Specialized Financing and Restructuring Group." My body would itch like hell inside one of my two worsted wool suits as I quietly listened to a Dead tape. The soft volume, coupled with the boredom I was experiencing daily, made things feel even worse.

But that was paradise compared to my "exciting days." I'd be about to count down the final moments before I could get on the subway uptown when a stressed first-year associate would pop in. Somehow, they always felt the need to wait until right before 5:00 PM and come by instead rather than calling.

"Thank God you're still here. Yeah, we're gonna be here all night. They've bumped up the closing to Friday and we need to get a distribution by tomorrow. It's hell on wheels."

The anger I felt upon hearing that admittedly lame expression suggested that I was far from happy at my job. This associate was only doing the bidding of the partner, who was completely beholden to the client. However, I didn't see that through my own frustration. Once again, I felt stuck and didn't know what to do about it.

I told the firm I was taking "an adult education class" when the Dead came to town and took my vacation days when they were on tour. But I missed my everyday freedom, so I called up DJ. After a long night of drinking, we hatched the idea of forming our own subway performance act.

"But Luca, I can only play the guitar passably and you don't play an instrument *at all.*"

"I'm not very good, but I'm not afraid to get up and sing."

"What kinds of tunes do think would make us any money?"

"What about TV theme songs from 1970s and '80s?"

I didn't know how much nostalgic appeal these tunes would have, but I figured they would be sure to get people's attention. More importantly, I knew all the words. Originally, we were going to call ourselves "The Salt Boys," like the male equivalent of the Spice Girls. DJ would be "Sea Salt" and I would obviously be "Kosher Salt."

"Luca, are you intentionally trying to scare people away?"

We settled on "Disco Volante" after the yacht-turned-hydrofoil from the Bond film *Thunderball.* I didn't think anyone would get it, but the word "disco" would at least get their attention. This would be especially important for our chosen venue, the 86th Street subway station. We wouldn't survive amongst the slackers in the East Village, but uptown there seemed to be a lot of "princesses" who might enjoy our kitschy vibe.

Veteran's Day fell on a Monday that year and felt like the perfect time to try out the act. I wouldn't even need to take a sick day as the firm was closed. I bought us a cheap microphone at Radio Shack to amplify us via my boombox. I taped together the lids from a few Banker's Boxes I stole from work to make a sign announcing our presence. DJ's guitar case lay open for the mountain of tips we hoped to get.

He began his countrified strumming as I turned on the microphone.

"Just the good ol' boys, never meaning no harm . . ."

Starting with the *Dukes of Hazzard*, my voice was far from on key. We weren't making the impression I hoped. Since the theme from *The Love Boat* was up next, I quickly made the decision to sing the rest of our set like a Vegas performer. I imagined myself as Bill Murray's "Nick Winters" from *Saturday Night Live*.

"Luuuuuuuvvvvvvvvhhhhh, exciting and NEW . . ." Now I noticed people starting to take notice. As soon as I sang "come aboard, we're expecting you," the tips started to come in. First there were quarters, then a few singles. By the time I got to *One Day at a Time*, I saw a five dollar bill staring back at me from the black interior of DJ's guitar case.

I looked over at DJ as I started moving away from the boom box. The microphone cord wasn't that long, but I thought I'd try to interact with those passing by. During the theme song from *Alice*, there were more than a few subway goers with their head down speeding by. But that only made me sing with more gusto.

"There's a neeeeeeeewww girl in town . . ."

At that moment, I felt a hand on my shoulder. I turned around to see one of New York's finest staring me in the eye.

"You guys have a permit to perform?"

"I didn't know we needed one," I sheepishly answered.

"You don't, unless you amplify yourselves."

I was about to point out how obscure and specific a law that was, but decided to point out that we planned to close with a reprise of the *Dukes of Hazzard* theme.

"Unless you want me to take that money you made, you'll get out of here right now."

That was the lone "Disco Volante" performance, but I couldn't believe how much fun we had. As we ran up the stairs towards Lexington Avenue, I also knew I'd eventually need to find a more fulfilling way to pay my bills.

FULL OF THE BLUES

LIKE MY JOB, my chosen neighborhood seemed like a good fit at first. But just like being a paralegal, the Upper East Side was just the result of me not having a better option. Money, DJ, and Rucker now lived in the East Village. Hollywood and I, on the other hand, lived on East 94th Street. I never really considered where in New York City I'd live after graduation. I foolishly assumed just being in Manhattan was enough. For the previous generation, anything north of 86th Street was considered ghetto. But by 1993, those next ten blocks had been gentrified into the perfect "starter" neighborhood. Every dry cleaner, diner, and video rental place seemed to cater to recent graduates who were just starting out in New York.

The center of this prefabricated community was the Normandie Court on 95th Street, appropriately nicknamed the "Dormandie." It was the only affordable housing that featured a gym, pool, and doorman. Every kid whose parents demanded that they live in a safe building ended up there. There was even a scale model of the complex itself displayed in the lobby, as if you needed any more evidence that this was the farthest thing possible from an authentic Manhattan living experience.

You could see the model under its stupid clear dome from the street. Every time I walked by, I reminded myself that at least my parents hadn't forced me to live there. But every time Hollywood and I went drinking on the Upper East Side, I was reminded of how much I didn't belong to this scene. I assumed bars would be my sanctuary. At Delt parties, all I had to do was walk into the lounge and I'd instantly find a girl to talk with. But these places all looked like a franchised version of a "college watering hole." The walls were covered with pennants of every Northeastern university as well as memorabilia from every local pro sports team. There would usually be an Irish flag somewhere as well, just to remind you that you were at a bar and that Irish people like to drink. The only thing I had going for me in the eyes of the girls I met in these places was my being Jewish. It only took a few minutes, however, for them to determine that I wasn't quite what they were looking for.

"You work at a law firm? That must be really great."

"How so?"

A confused pause followed, as if I should already know.

"You'll get great references for law school and maybe even a job when you graduate."

"Yeah, but I don't think I'll ever go to law school."

"Oh . . ."

The only thing "professional" about me was the fact that I had a steady job at a respected firm. I thought I was fighting conformity by staying true to myself, but had actually returned to being the "fake rebel" of my middle school years. I grew a beard, thinking it was some outlaw gesture. All it really did, however, was barely mask the fact that my drinking was finally starting to cause me to gain weight. It seemed like everything was harder than it had been at college. The more I realized this, however, the less I was willing to do about it. At this point, I was probably doing everything I could to ensure that I wouldn't meet anyone. Even the few scattered hookups I had felt pointless. I was so far down that I couldn't even appreciate them for the welcome indulgences they were.

It was after one too many of these frustrating evenings out that I decided to finally call Kerry. Hollywood and I had just thrown back some whiskey shots. It was Thursday night and the Upper East Kids were getting ready to start their weekend. I looked around the bar as music blared overhead. It was "Good" by Better Than Ezra. The clanging bass line gave way to lyrics about not being too proud to call or write someone a letter. I was already thinking about Kerry and this sealed the deal. It's also a really catchy song.

It couldn't hurt to ring her up. We hadn't spoken since graduation.

Fuck it. I decided to tell Hollywood I was heading back to the apartment.

It wasn't as if I hadn't been close to calling before this night. Every failed attempt to pick up a girl reminded me that I didn't have put up with this shit not so long ago. I had a girlfriend and everything was great. Of course, I spent the second half of my senior year suppressing the fact that we were drifting apart. During that time, I had gotten in the habit of acting like I didn't care what anyone thought of me. I was now becoming a parody of my college self. When things had been good with Kerry, everything felt right. I felt right. She was living in Buffalo. There was no way she could have found someone new.

I cracked open a Rolling Rock when I got back to the apartment. Hollywood was making headway with a cute blonde and probably wouldn't be back for a while. He definitely wouldn't approve of me calling Kerry. In his world, things were that black and white. If it was over, that was it. It didn't matter why and there weren't any loose ends.

I called the only number I had, her parents' house.

"This is Rob, Ms. McNaughton. You know, from Kerry's graduation?"

"Oh yeah . . ." There was something in her voice that made me uneasy. It wasn't just that we had met over a year and a half ago. Her mom said Kerry was now living in her own apartment. Had she met someone? What if she was living with them, just like *we'd* once talked about? I had to know, so I punched in the number.

"Hullo?" That raspy voice still got me.

"Kerry, it's Rob. What's going on?" I was trying to sound casual even as I could tell it appeared anything but.

"Rob. I can't believe you called. Are you still living in New York City?"

"Of course. You obviously got your own place. Did you ever find that teaching job?"

"I did, actually. But do you really want to catch up right now?"

"Why not?"

"First off, you never really do things casually. Plus, now I'm kind of . . ."

Shit. I knew where this was going.

"You're seeing someone, aren't you?"

"Yeah."

That was when I checked out of the conversation, even though it went on for a few minutes. I think I told her I was happy for her and gave her my number. Even in my completely numbed state, I knew we'd never talk again. Did I actually think that calling her would somehow transport me back to the summer before junior year? I was probably hoping rather than thinking, as sad as that sounds.

It took me a couple of days to recover from that call. It had been almost a year since I graduated college, but I knew now it was really over. I hadn't really done anything since leaving Rochester, but it wasn't until talking to Money one night that I realized how much I'd let myself slip. We were having beers at McSwiggan's, a nice dive bar in the east 20s.

"Luca, man, you don't look happy these days. What's up?"

I knew what he was getting at, but tried to deflect by pointing to my facial hair.

"I'll probably shave it off at some point."

"Not the beard, although I don't think looking like Silent Bob from *Clerks* is ever a good thing. You just seem pissed off. We're young and living in the greatest city in the world!"

"Yeah, but my job's going nowhere."

"So find another one."

"I wish it was that easy. You guys live downtown and seem to have fun all the time. The Upper East Side sucks."

"True, but you don't have to live there forever. You sound like a guy in his 40s with all this responsibility. You need to lighten up while it all plays out. I've also heard your rap with chicks. You used to just be sarcastic and funny, but now you sound bitter and desperate. No one wants to be around that."

He was right. I had to find a way to enjoy the uncertainty of life again. Fortunately, I got a six-month stay that fall on figuring out my future and it came from the least expected place imaginable.

The Chargers finally made it to the Super Bowl.

FOLLOWING THE DREAM

I SHOULD HAVE LISTENED to the lessons learned from all those *Twilight Zone* episodes (and even the passing thought that a third *Godfather* film could be a good idea) that all fulfilled wishes come at a price. At the very least, I should have specified that I wanted a Super Bowl win after watching the Chargers fall a game short for two straight years as a kid.

They were only a season removed from being in the playoffs, but the team let much of their marquee talent sign with other teams as free agents during the summer of 1994. They signed guys with the money they saved, but they seemed more like "role players" than the stars the team had let walk.

I was convinced these personnel moves would backfire, so I began calling the front office in San Diego from my cubicle at work. This way, I could bill the calls to a client. I never got through to Chargers ownership or management on the phone, but instead got an intern from the PR department.

"Look," I said, "it's great that you are filling holes on the roster. But those are just the holes the general manager is creating by letting better guys sign with other teams."

"And who are you, exactly?"

"I'm just a passionate fan calling from New York City."

"New York City? I'll certainly pass your thoughts on to the GM."

Just in case he didn't keep his word, I also left countless voicemails after hours. At least it gave me something to do all those nights stuck at work. As long as I kept billing different clients for the calls, I'd be safe from detection.

The season opened on a Sunday night in Denver. The Chargers fell behind 21-6 to John Elway and the Broncos and it seemed like all my offseason fears were well-founded. However, the Bolts came back and took a three-point lead late in the fourth quarter, only to give Elway back the ball with one more shot to finish them off. Of course, he drove them down the field as he so often did and had them set up for the winning score.

Then something strange happened. Just as Elway cocked back his arm to throw what would undoubtedly be the winning touchdown pass, the ball slipped out. It landed directly in the hands of the Chargers' best player, linebacker Junior Seau. He hauled it in and then dropped both feet in bounds. He sprinted to midfield and spiked the ball to suggest that maybe this year would actually be different.

By the time the Dead came to the Garden for six nights that October, the Chargers were 6-0 and on the cover of *Sports Illustrated* as the NFL's last undefeated team. They stumbled a bit after that, but at 9-5 they had an opportunity to clinch their division against the Jets in New Jersey in December. I dragged myself out to the Meadowlands after a long night partying just to see it happen firsthand. After capturing the AFC West with a 21-6 win, I decided to stop by the team bus. I spotted General

Manager (and future Hall of Famer) Bobby Beathard and extended my hand.

"Thanks for letting me leave all those messages and for not following any of my suggestions."

As he got on to board, he turned around and I was sure for a moment that he recognized my voice.

The team faced Dan Marino and the Dolphins in the first round of the playoffs. This was the same team that blew them out of the postseason 31-0 two seasons before. The Chargers immediately fell behind 22-6 by the half. The players were reportedly so pissed that one of them hit the walls of the locker room so hard that it caused the lights to go out on the opponents' side. Apparently, the Dolphins weren't able to conduct any meetings before coming back out for the second half. These were the kind of things that usually happened *to* the Chargers.

The Bolts came all the way back in the second half to lead by two, but they also gave Marino the ball with enough time to get the Dolphins close enough for the winning field goal. It was a 49-yarder, but their kicker was one of the league's best and had made eight of his ten attempts from that range during the year.

Fortunately, I had more than enough alcohol and company to calm my nerves as Miami lined up to try to win it and end the Chargers' season. Money and DJ had made the trip uptown to watch the game at my apartment. My buddy Eric, a Chargers fan from my days in Chappaqua, was also there. Richie, a guy I had met at the bar where I regularly watched games, joined us as well. I took a shot of whiskey and mumbled "justice is coming," the tagline from that year's film *Tombstone*. I had adopted it as my mantra for the season. The image of the Earp Brothers and Doc Holliday taking care of business at the OK Corral somehow connected to my belief that the Chargers meant to finally win. As if that wasn't enough to bring some positive mojo, I was blasting the soundtrack to Oliver Stone's *JFK* and screaming, "Let justice be done though the heavens fall!" from the film.

Eric, a sketch comedian who was on his way towards being an extremely successful writer for late-night television, burst out laughing as he did a shot with me.

"Rob, you're out of your mind right now. But I love it."

What could I say? I really needed the Chargers to continue to find the magic at that moment. After the kick fluttered wide of the upright, I ran out on to the fire escape, ripped off my shirt, and threw it down Third Avenue. Since it was January and cold, I instantly regretted my decision. Fortunately, my Chargers flag was tied to the railing. I wrapped it around myself like Rocky Balboa in Russia as everyone came out to check on me. I couldn't believe the Chargers were one game from the Super Bowl. They had failed twice in that spot in the Dan Fouts days, but this felt different.

That feeling was reinforced by the bourbon-fueled euphoria I was experiencing. However, Stan Humphries seemed like the guy who could do it. I turned to Richie, with whom I'd never hung out outside of a sports bar and asked him if he'd ever been to Pittsburgh.

"Are you kidding? Did you see how the Steelers destroyed the Browns yesterday? Plus that crowd is more than a little hostile." He was right. This was the Steelers' best shot at regaining Super Bowl glory since their dynasty of the 1970s. By the next day, they were favored by nine points, which was the largest spread in conference title game history. Jeff Daniels, who would be hosting *Saturday Night Live* that weekend, told viewers to "take Pittsburgh and the points" in the promos. Even Harry Dunne from *Dumb and Dumber* was betting against us.

None of this kept me from booking a flight to a place I had never been with a guy I had never seen outside of a sports bar. I tuned out all negativity that week. The only decorations I had in my cubicle at work were news clippings from all the Chargers' big wins that year, along with some pictures of the Dead. I now added a seating chart of Three Rivers Stadium with a bulls-eye drawn on it in Steelers colors. My entire workspace looked like the lair of a madman.

After Richie and I walked from our hotel the morning of the game, we could see the stadium over the chain link fence around the parking lot. It looked to be rising out of the mist just as it did in all those classic NFL Films chronicling the Steelers' four Super Bowl wins. The lot was even louder than I expected and as we approached we could see why. The Chargers' bus was pulling in and people were throwing eggs at it. There were even black and gold clad fans running towards it and trying to push it over. This was going to require more liquid courage than I thought.

I had my fraternity wineskin around my neck overflowing with Jim Beam and a twelve-pack of Pittsburgh's own Iron City Ale under my arm. It didn't seem like the lot was a safe place to root for the opposition, so I told Richie we should head into the stadium.

"Rob, there's no way they let us in with that."

"Look around you. I'm wearing a Stan Humphries jersey while the fans are trying to capsize the fucking bus. I think they'll let us through the gates with *anything* if we're prepared for the consequences inside."

Sure enough, the ushers took one look at me and waved us through.

"It's your funeral," I heard one of them say.

We didn't get too much abuse from the fans because the Steelers led by 10 points in the third quarter. Then Stan Humphries shocked the stadium into silence by throwing two 43-yard touchdown passes to put the Bolts up 17-13. The first one was to tight end Alfred Pupunu, who had somehow gotten lost in the Steelers secondary and the second pass was truly right out of a movie. The barely mobile Humphries barely escaped a sack and was hit late after releasing the ball. It hung in the air for so long it seemed to be wobbling in slow motion. When I say it wobbled, it looked like a top that was about to skid to a stop. However, it sped back up as it came hurtling into the hands of receiver Tony Martin, who had simultaneously jumped off the turf to snatch it.

I screamed downward in excitement not only because of my hostile surroundings. I knew that the Steelers would have the chance to win the game with their own touchdown. This would not only put them in the Super Bowl, but help avoid their being upset by a mammoth underdog. Games like this always seemed to come down to the defense needing to make one last stand. By now, we had finished all the beer and were pretty deep into the whiskey. Besides a few trips to the bathroom, I hadn't left my seat all afternoon. Once again, I was grateful that my buzz kept me from feeling the anxiety I knew the moment warranted.

Of course, the Steelers drove down to the Chargers 9-yard line. They had enough time for four chances to win before time ran out. After two incomplete passes, they ran it down to the 3. Junior Seau, who was playing through a pinched nerve in his neck, somehow held his ground to keep the ball carrier from scoring. It was down to one play.

The Steelers tried a pass over the middle. Linebacker Dennis Gibson, one of the role players signed in the offseason, reached over the shoulder of the receiver to bat it down. When the ball hit the turf, I realized that the Chargers had done it. *They finally made it to the fucking Super Bowl.*

I felt like I was walking on air during my flight home when I wasn't throwing up in the bathroom. All that Super Bowl hype I endured every year would finally be about *my* team. The next day was Martin Luther King Day. DJ and I went to the afternoon Knicks game even though I still hadn't slept or even changed my clothes. As we walked around the Garden trying to find our seats, I heard a smattering of applause."FUCK THE STEELERS!"

"GET 'EM, HUMPHRIES!" The one thing Jets and Giants fans agreed on was that they both hated the heavy favorites. By the time we reached our seats, the crowd was cheering so loudly that I thought the Knicks must have made a big play. A few

minutes later, a correspondent from legendary WNEW-FM DJ
Pat St. John's morning show came over to us.

"I assume from the jersey that you're a Chargers fan. Would
you say you're a long-suffering one?"

"Is there any other kind?"

The 49ers were already installed as the biggest favorite in
Super Bowl history at 18½ points. But after the last two miracu-
lous wins, there was no way that the Bolts could lose now. I had
to be there for the last leg of this magical journey, no matter
what it took.

DRUNK ON SUPER SUNDAY

THE GAME, TO BE PLAYED that year in Miami, wasn't
for two weeks. I had some time to figure out how to get myself
there, but I'd need to do it alone. Richie had to get back to his
job after the Pittsburgh trip and Eric's sketch comedy group was
performing that weekend. The fact I couldn't get anyone to join
me should have given me some pause, but it only made me more
determined. At least, I would have an easier time tracking down
a single ticket, or so I thought.

There was no internet yet to help, but I eventually found
a scalping agency that had a ticket for $850. Unless you won a
season-ticket lottery from either of the teams playing or the one
hosting the game, there is no way to buy a ticket for the Super
Bowl. The entire market for the average fan was "secondary."
This was the biggest purchase of my life to this point, but I saw
no way to back out now. The scalper on the phone asked me
which team I was going to see.

"The Chargers, of course."

He didn't respond before taking down my credit card

information. His silence should have been another sign. There was a reason that the 49ers were the biggest (to this day) favorites in Super Bowl history as they had assembled a once-in-a-generation "megateam." They signed a ton of talent to short-term contracts and deferred much of the money to signing bonuses in order to stay under the NFL's just-instituted salary cap. It was the opposite approach to what the Chargers had done that season. The NFL would later fine San Francisco $600,000 and dock them a couple of draft picks for their "circumvention." But that was long after the fact. The 49ers were heading into Super Bowl XXIX with a squad stocked with eight free agent acquisitions, including six Pro Bowlers. Superstar cornerback Deion Sanders agreed to take a one-year deal for almost nothing just to join them and get his Super Bowl ring. It was *that* likely he'd get it. The Niners had even beaten the Chargers by 23 points a month earlier in San Diego with "Neon Deion" returning an interception 90 yards for the final touchdown.

I knew all this when I committed to going to the game. Like the passengers in *Airplane!*, however, I bought my ticket and knew what I was getting into. I didn't give up my quest even after I realized that getting a hotel room near the Super Bowl is almost as tough a task as scoring a ticket for the game. Fortunately, my friend Greg's family had a condominium in Boca Raton with an entire floor they kept vacant for renters. He had told me before the playoffs started that if the Chargers somehow made it to the Super Bowl, I could stay there. I don't think he thought there was much chance of that happening because he and his fiancée were already flying down for a romantic weekend when I took him up on his offer.

I received my first ever jury duty summons for the day after the game and was proud to be able to write in my excuse as "going to the Super Bowl." I wasn't nearly as proud at what my plane ticket cost, but the free lodging made me falsely believe I was coming out even. I picked up my rental car at the Fort Lauderdale airport after the flight. Greg and his fiancée wouldn't be back from dinner for a few hours yet, so I pulled over to grab a bottle of whiskey on the way. It turned out to be a smart move because afterwards the security guard at the gate told me that he couldn't let me through until they got back. After he saw the disappointment on my face, he softened the blow by telling me I could wait the parking lot adjacent to the security both.

After having a drink in my car, I decided to knock on the booth's window. The guard was a little hesitant at first when I asked if I could wait with him, but he relented after I flashed my bottle of whiskey. He had a microwave in there and cooked up a frozen pizza up for both of us to share. As we were waiting, I noticed a photocopied picture taped to the wall of what appeared to be a man in his seventies. The caption read:

"SOLOMON FEINBERG IS NOT TO BE ALLOWED INSIDE THE DEVELOPMENT UNDER ANY CIRCUM-STANCES."

I had to find out more.

"What did he do to get banned from this place?"

"Who, Solomon? He just likes to stand outside the window while some of the old ladies get undressed. It sounds funny to say, but the residents don't like it too much."

"How do you know his name if he doesn't even live here?"

"He used to. He was even the condo president."

"I guess you never know," I said.

"You fuckin' said it."

Greg and his fiancée came home a little while after we finished the pizza. As they pulled up to the gate, I could hear my friend start to inquire as to my whereabouts.

"I see my friend's car over there, but . . ."

It was just at that moment that he spotted me inside the security hut enjoying Jim Beam and Ellio's pizza. After showing me to my room for the weekend, Greg had a quick drink with me to laugh about it.

"But seriously, Rob, I don't think you should drive tomorrow."

I agreed but not just because of the drinking. I was as amped up as I'd ever been for something. Whatever awaited me tomorrow had been building since that day at the bus stop when I promised to always be a Chargers fan.

Luckily, there was a special train and bus route I could take to the stadium. By the time I got off the train, I had a pretty nice bourbon buzz going. As I waited for the shuttle bus, I felt a wheelchair pull up beside me. In it was a guy wearing a Chargers hat and an old army jacket. He eyed the Humphries jersey and the wineskin under my arm and asked if he could get a swig of the wine.

"It's not wine. It's Jim Beam."

"Even better."

We shared a couple of pulls before the bus arrived. He was lifted on board first and I followed him to the back of the bus. On the way to the game, he asked how I'd become a Chargers fan. I told him my story.

"From that day on, I pledged . . ."

Keith, my new friend, wasn't freaked out at all. The more I talked, the more his eyes widened in appreciation. When a couple of other "Boltheads" overheard me talking, one of them screamed out:

"You're not even from San Diego? Why'd you come to the Super Bowl?"

Keith immediately came to my defense.

"Hey, this guy knows more about the Chargers than anyone I've ever met! He *chose* to become a fan. He was just in Pittsburgh, for Christ's sakes. Can any of you say the same? Yeah, I didn't fucking think so."

When we got to the stadium, I thanked Keith for having my back.

"I really think today's the day," I added. "Justice is coming."

I had almost finished the contents of the wineskin and decided to head for the gate. On the way in, I saw a fellow Chargers fan offering free face painting. I had always been opposed to the practice, even before the famous *Seinfeld* episode mocked it. Given the circumstances, however, I figured I'd break my own rule.

When the girl let me look at myself in her hand-held mirror, I thought I looked like someone who'd eaten the brown acid at Woodstock. Instead of swirls and flowers on my face, though, there was blue and gold with a lightning bolt streaking diagonally across it. It looked just like the most famous of all Grateful Dead logos, but in Charger colors. Of course, I had no idea how hot the paint would feel in the Florida sun. My sweat quickly made the whole thing look like a terrifying mess.

I could only imagine what I looked like as the game progressed. It was a total bloodbath from the start. The Chargers committed a facemask penalty on the first play and the 49ers started at their own 41-yard line. On the third play, San Francisco threw a 44-yard touchdown, which was the quickest score in Super Bowl history up to that point.

After forcing the Chargers to punt, the 49ers threw another long touchdown and led 14-0 after only five minutes. San Francisco set a number of records that day. For one, quarterback Steve Young threw six touchdown passes. At least each one stung a little less than the one before it, thankfully and sadly. It all happened so quickly, that I never had the chance to have my hopes dashed. The Bolts were technically within a touchdown at one point, down 14-7. But it never felt that close and the Niners quickly pulled away and went on to win the game, 49-26. The scary thing is that it felt like we had lost by even more than 23 points.

I stayed until the final snap, but only out of loyalty and the astronomical amount of money I had spent to witness this disaster. As the San Francisco fans celebrated, I headed towards the exit. As I rounded the perimeter of the stadium and moved towards the shuttle bus, I heard a familiar song. It sounded like Dickey Betts' guitar coupled with the voice of Gregg Allman, but was even clearer than a live recording. I saw a tent outside the stadium where I thought the sound was coming from. This had to be the best Allman Brothers Band tribute act of all time. When I peeked inside the tent, however, I realized it was the actual Allmans. They were in the beginning of "Soulshine," and Gregg was singing about the stars not shining bright and feeling like you've lost your way.

Security saw me peeking in and immediately asked me to move along. It looked like everyone inside was wearing 49er colors. Then again, who else would be in the mood to celebrate at that moment? Not only had we gotten blown out in the Super Bowl, one of my favorite bands was playing a private party for those enjoying it.

As I got onto the shuttle bus, I thought of Bruce Springsteen's question from "The River:" If your dream goes unfulfilled, is it something even worse than a lie?

All I ever wanted was for the Chargers to make the Super Bowl to validate my years of suffering. I had never considered how it would feel to *lose* the game.

Of course, the pain eventually subsided and I had myself believing that they would make it back soon enough. They were a young team, after all. Unfortunately, it seemed like the Bolts had exhausted all their magic that season. Maybe they'd made a deal with the devil since eight players from that team would die in the next 18 years. Two were found dead in their homes (enlarged heart and overdose), two others died in car crashes, and one was even *struck by lightning.* The worst death of all was when Hall of Famer Junior Seau committed suicide in 2012. While his death brought a lot of attention to the disturbing propensity of the brain disease CTE in former players, it also ensured that when you search for "1994 Chargers" on the web the word *curse* will automatically pop up. So not only did my team get destroyed in record-setting fashion the one time they reached football's promised land, but they are now also known for being marked for death like the kids in the *Final Destination* movies.

When I got back to the office that Tuesday, I took down all my Chargers clippings from my cubicle and put them in my drawer. I knew I couldn't just quit my job, especially with all the debt I'd accumulated over the last weekend. But looking at the bare burlap walls while doing the same mindless tasks day after day finally seemed too much to bear.

I needed to get out of there, but didn't know how to do it or where I'd go to.

Almost Ablaze at the Creek

"BEFORE WE GO OVER YOUR REVIEWS, you need to ask yourself a question. Do you even *want* to be here anymore?"

This was my two-year performance review at the law firm. I wasn't completely surprised by this question. At this point, corporate legal assistants either went on to law school or were content being paralegals for the long haul. I knew I wasn't interested in either option, so it no longer made sense for me to work there. That wouldn't be how my parents saw it, however. Without the job I hated, I couldn't live in the city and I'd lose my medical benefits. I decided to play dumb with the Legal Assistant Coordinator as she conducted the review.

"I'm confused," I said. "What did the reviews actually say?"

She grabbed one off her desk. "Rob is very intelligent and seemingly would be much happier doing something else."

I couldn't disagree with that assessment, but my vocational dissatisfaction was becoming more and more evident to all. She went on to explain that I was being let go, but would have two months to find a new job. After that, the firm would allow me to file for unemployment and I could buy insurance through a COBRA plan. I didn't know how any of this worked, but knew I'd better update my resume immediately. After telling my parents the news, I quickly realized that this would be the only way I would ever leave. I was obsessively fanatical, extremely loyal, but also unwilling to admit to myself when something was clearly not working. I started going into the office on Saturdays to work on my resume since I didn't yet have a computer. When I got to the "additional interests" section, it occurred to me that nothing I did outside of class during college would be appropriate to list. I had written for my high school paper and my essays were the only thing that saved my ass from academic probation in college. How could I make something of that skill?

In the same office where my mind had stagnated for two years, I started putting together a writing portfolio. I also started an online newsletter about the Chargers called *Justice Is Coming*. Since these were the days before blogs, I needed my buddy Eric to show me how to distribute it on the internet. I submitted reviews of recent Dead shows to the "fanzines" and even wrote a few special interest pieces for a few of the city's free papers.

I knew I would still have to find a way to pay my bills, but it felt good to use my brain again. With the ability to file for unemployment on the horizon, I felt a little less stressed about my situation when the Dead's summer tour arrived. After dates in Vermont, New Jersey, and Washington, I was eagerly awaiting my one real "destination show." I was finally going to Deer Creek.

Deer Creek Amphitheatre in Noblesville, Indiana was the type of place the band had mostly outgrown by 1995. It had only had about 6,000 seats and room for another 18,000 on the lawn. Venues like that, especially on the East Coast, attracted far too many Deadheads by this point. The only reason Deer Creek was still an available option was because it was in the middle of the country. The band clearly enjoyed playing there and the shows there were some of the strongest each summer. One of my fellow

Delts whose shock of orange hair and accompanying moustache earned him the nickname Yosemite Sam (Yo for short) told me he had lawn tickets for both of the Deer Creek shows that were scheduled for July 2nd and 3rd. I knew I had to make the trip.

A plane ticket to Indianapolis wasn't all that expensive, even on July 4th weekend. Plus, I booked the cheapest motel I could find through the firm's in-house travel agency. I figured I might as well use those privileges while I still could. I was about to leave work that Friday when I got a message that Yo couldn't get there until the following morning. It was too late for me to change my flight, but figured I could occupy myself for a night. As I left work, I noticed a magnum of champagne in one of the vacant conference rooms. It was a closing gift for one of the firm's major clients. I didn't really like champagne, but liked the idea that some associate would be manically looking for it. I shoved it in my carry-on bag for the trip to Indy along with a Montecristo cigar I spotted.

My flight went smoothly and I was even able to share a few drinks with other Deadheads travelling for the shows. I hailed a cab pretty easily at the airport and I asked the driver if he knew how to get to the Imperial Gardens motel. I immediately started to get a very strange vibe.

"You in the service?"

I was thirty pounds overweight and wearing a Dead shirt. I was as close to being a member of the armed forces as I was to being on the soccer team in college. "No, I'm not. Why would you ask?"

"Usually the ones who go out to the Gardens are servicemen in town for the night."

It only took a few minutes to get to the Imperial Gardens, but it seemed like another planet. It was like a trailer park without the trailers. Near the motel's offices, there were three kids smoking blunts on the brick railing staring at me as I got out of the cab.

I had a sinking feeling that there weren't going to be any other Deadheads staying there.

I did, however, quickly understand the appeal of the Imperial Gardens for service members. There was a sign over the front desk saying that rooms were available for hourly rates. If you couldn't find female company for the night, there were also VCRs behind the desk clerk for rent. I also saw a bunch of titles scribbled on formerly blank tapes, with the first being *The Princess and the Penis*. Although I did wonder for a second what the plot could possibly be about, I decided it was best to get into my room as quickly as possible.

As I climbed the exterior staircase, I heard, "Sugar, you need company?" off in the distance. After closing the door, I immediately bolted it shut. I slid the chain in place as well even though all it did was remind me how often those things broke when someone kicked the door open in the movies. Everything about the room made me think that it could actually be a possibility. There was wood paneling on the walls, the likes of which I hadn't seen since the 1970s. An old Sony Trinitron was bolted onto the dresser. I supposed that if you opted for the VCR rental, they'd have to bolt that down too. With a weird combination of dread and fascination, I went to check out the bathroom. I assumed that would serve as a good barometer of how much trouble I had gotten myself into.

The shower head was mounted at a height that only a "little person" could enjoy and the bottom of the tub was covered in faded orange stains. I decided to lie down on the bed, but didn't dare peel back the blanket. I felt like sandpaper, but I knew I made the right call when I spotted the little circled shaped marks in the ceiling. I assumed they were bullet holes but didn't stand up to get a closer look. The bed would probably have collapsed anyway.

Every instinct told me to get the fuck out of there, but heading into the Indianapolis night didn't seem so smart either. I had no idea what time it was, but I decided instantly to try to go to bed. I put my headphones on and cranked up a Dead tape on my Walkman. I was actually able to fall asleep pretty quickly.

I woke up in the middle of the night to the phone ringing. The sign behind the desk said that you needed to prepay in order to make outgoing calls, but incoming calls were apparently complimentary. I fumbled in the dark and grabbed the receiver.

"Yo, is Willie there?"

"Uh, I think you have the wrong number," I replied.

"You mean Willie moved out?"

Before he could ask if Willie left a forwarding address, I hung up. I took the phone off the hook and left the receiver on the night stand. Sunday morning couldn't come soon enough. I saw a liquor store within walking distance on the cab ride in. As soon as I thought it might be open, I decided to make a break for it.

I knew I'd need bourbon if I was going to sleep in that room for another night. As I approached the shelf for the Jim Beam, I noticed something different about the bottle. It looked cloudy, like it was made of plastic. I picked it up and realized that it actually was.

I was awestruck. The tag on the shelf read "Jim Beam 750 ml Lightweight Traveler." I turned the bottle around to read the label. *"Made from the highest quality ingredients, Jim Beam is the world's finest bourbon. To drink Jim Beam is not only to taste its full bourbon character, but its rich American heritage. It's perfect to take on the go for parties, meetings, and gatherings."* I couldn't imagine a meeting you could bring Jim Beam into, but I clearly needed to step up my job search. I bought two bottles and headed back to the hotel.

I also picked up some breakfast at McDonald's and waited for Yo to show up. I cracked open one of the Travelers and turned on the TV. Fortunately, 1977's *The Warriors* was on. It was about three quarters through the movie when I heard the knock at the door. The combination of a great cult movie and the whiskey made me forget that I had shoved a chair under the doorknob for protection. When I opened the door, Yo saw the chair.

"What kind of place did you book us in? Wait, is that a plastic bottle of Beam in your hand?"

"Which question do you want me to answer first? The second one's a lot easier."

"Just grab your stuff and let's head to the lot."

The Deer Creek Amphitheatre was everything Deadheads said it was. After taking a two-lane road through literal cornfields, we parked. It was in a particularly scenic location, with a long grass parking lot abutting the creek. I leaned up against the trunk of the rental car to take it all in. I didn't see any deer, but assumed they took July off. I reached into the Styrofoam cooler and found the bottle of champagne I swiped from work. I popped it open and decided to take a stroll around the lot.

By 1995, the parking lots of Grateful Dead concerts were no longer safe spaces for illicit activity. Local law enforcement even had actual sting operations set up by this point at many of the cities the band played in. I once saw cops in Charlotte putting on long-haired wigs and tie-dyes just to try to make some pre-show busts. Simultaneously, there were more people than ever coming to Dead shows only for the now-legendary party. Many of them weren't even trying to see the show, just "the scene." They wanted to get their kicks, consequences be damned. Two opposite trends were destined for a collision course. Sadly, Deer Creek was where everything came to a head.

As I walked the around the lot that Sunday, I already could feel the desperation in the air. People weren't there just for the lot, they wanted to get into the show. There were the usual characters with their fingers in the air looking for an extra ticket, only twice as many as usual. When someone actually had one to sell, I heard more than one ticket seeker demand that it be "miracled" to them free of charge. Dead shows now seemed to be a right, rather than a privilege.

I saw a kid pass me by looking for spare change so he could stay on tour. That wasn't unusual, so I kept on walking. That's when he circled back and charged at me.

"What do you mean you don't have any change!"

"Huh?"

"Fucking yuppie, look at yourself!"

I didn't even know people used that term any more. I looked at him and noticed that he had brand new Birkenstock sandals and the $35 tour shirts they sold inside the shows. He could have easily passed for a Pi Phi at Rochester.

"You're walking around the lot with your champagne. I bet you've got a ticket for the show."

I forgot that I still had the magnum in my hand. I didn't think explaining that I stole it from a *real* yuppie would make any difference.

"Well, yeah, but . . ."

"Do you even like the Dead? How many times have you seen them?"

"Tonight will be 138." I thought that would shut him up.

"Yeah, fucking yuppie, *of course* you have. How else could you afford all those tickets?"

This kid was probably from some middle-class suburb, just like me. I might have been older than him, but there was no way I was going to sit here and defend my right to be at what I could never had guessed would be my final Grateful Dead concert. I sure as shit wasn't going to speak for "the Establishment" that I was no part of.

"If I'm a yuppie, where's my yuppie job? Where's my yuppie wife? Where's my yuppie family?" I just walked away and decided to tell Yo we should just head in. There was nothing left for me out here. This entire incident should have served as an omen, like when Mick Jagger got punched in the face by a fan on the way into Altamont. "I hate you. You're so fucked," the guy supposedly told him.

It was a good thing we decided to get on line. They had metal detectors in front of the gates, which I had never seen at a show before. I saw similar looks of confusion on Deadheads' faces during a pat down better suited for a super max prison. Deer Creek was supposed to be a haven, not whatever this was.

The show started normally enough. The band opened with "Here Comes Sunshine" with the houselights still on. The lights also stayed on for the next song, which seemed odd. Our spot on the lawn was so great, however, that I didn't question anything. I had never been so close to the stage with a lawn ticket and the slope of the grass was so gradual that there wasn't a bad spot anywhere. There was a ton of empty grass behind us leading to a wooden fence right out of *Tom Sawyer.* I couldn't imagine it would keep too many people out of the show, but also couldn't imagine a situation where it would have to.

"I guess a lot of people are stuck outside," Yo said.

"It's better for us," I replied, since we had so much room to enjoy the music.

Every now and then, however, I'd hear a roar from behind us. It sounded like some giant beast was beyond the fence. At first, I thought it might be the Jim Beam playing tricks on me, but it was definitely getting louder. When the band covered Bob Dylan's "Desolation Row," the roar became a monstrous cheer. Yo and I moved back a little on the lawn to see what was going on. In one of those cosmic coincidences that seemed to only happen at a Dead show, Bob Weir was singing about the riot squad being restless and needing somewhere to go when people started jumping the fence.

We couldn't actually see what happened next, but people were screaming, "they broke through!" within seconds. This wasn't all that surprising since sticking it to the man had always been a part of the hippie ethos. Forcing concerts to become free festivals dated back to Woodstock.

I looked back to the stage to see if the band was going to

make some sort of an acknowledgement. The lights were still on, which I assumed would now be the norm for the rest of the show. They kept playing, so I wondered if they were even aware of what had happened. Yo and I tried to back up a bit more but more people were filling up the lawn now. Any idea I had about moving towards the chaos evaporated when I saw people were running from security while holding pieces of the fence in their hands. One guy almost trampled the baby sitting on the blanket in front of us before her parents swooped her up. This was starting to get really ugly. Now I wondered if the band was afraid to say anything or stop playing to keep the crowd from really rioting. They played a more few songs before ending the set.

During the break, I heard different accounts of what had caused the crowd tear the fence down.

"The cops let this attack dog go after this guy with dreads and that's what did it."

"No, man. The dog *belonged* to the dreads guy and they were trying to cuff him. When the dog ran off, he ran and they went after him with batons. People were rushing up the hill towards the fence to check it all out."

We couldn't move back for the second set, so we decided to stay put. There was no official announcement, but we figured we'd get the real story afterawrds. As we walked back to the car, we saw what was left of the fence. The jagged shards that remained in place seemed like a metaphor for the anger I experienced in the lot. We were about to take a closer look at the wreckage when our eyes were filled with the remnants of the tear gas.

Suddenly, the Imperial Gardens didn't seem quite so dangerous. I figured we'd better head to the show earlier the next day. When we got to the lot the following afternoon, however, there were sawhorse-style signs saying it was cancelled altogether.

"No way," I told Yo. "The band has never cancelled a show because of Deadheads."

But it was true. When I saw all the news reports after

returning to New York, I learned that people were throwing bottles at the cops and lighting the security golf carts on fire. To top things off, Jerry Garcia had apparently gotten a death threat before the show. He refused to cancel, but that was the reason the houselights were on. It was never confirmed exactly what had caused the riot, but the amount of security needed for the death threat undoubtedly left a lot less to patrol the fence. Still, who could have predicted the cops would need to defend it like a medieval moat?

Entertainment Weekly and MTV ran stories in the weeks to follow about how this would be the end of Dead tours or how there was a curse following the band and its fans. That seemed like a stretch, even after Deer Creek. I was more than a little relieved when the fall tour was announced later that month, even though I knew I'd be out of the job by September. As I bought my ticket for the six shows that fall at Madison Square Garden, I hoped I'd have a plan together by then.

THE BROKEN ANGEL SINGS NO MORE

UNFORTUNATELY, I STILL HADN'T FOUND a solution once August rolled around. My parents generously agreed to pay the premiums of my COBRA health plan, but I knew I didn't have much time. It had been two years since I'd graduated and I felt no closer to figuring shit out. At my exit interview on the Wednesday of my last week, the firm at least told me they would give me a positive reference. Of course, I had no idea what job I would use that reference for.

I got back to my desk afterwards and figured I'd just pretend to work for the remainder of the day. It's not like it mattered at this point. As far as I knew, I couldn't be fired twice from the same job. I sat down and noticed that the voicemail light on my phone was pulsing at what seemed like double time. Who knew it could even do that?

I punched in my password and the first message was from the switchboard operator telling me that I had gotten fifteen outside voicemails in the last thirty minutes. My mailbox was full and all subsequent callers would hear an automated message explaining this. I had no idea why I was suddenly so popular. I had only submitted a few resumes for temp paralegal jobs at that point and never used my work phone as a contact number anyway. This had to be bad news.

My first fear was that I had suffered a family emergency, but then fifteen people wouldn't have called me within a half hour. That left only one possibility:

Jerry Garcia had died.

The first message was from Money, who never called me at work. "I just heard about Jerry on the radio. I'm sorry, man."

If he was calling, it had to be all over the news. The rest of the messages were from assorted friends, Delts, and relatives. I couldn't believe that many people even knew where I worked. The last message was from my dad:

"Rob, your mom and I know this must be really hard. We know how important this band was to you and I'm really happy you took me to that concert a few years back. I guess it had to end sometime. Call us when you're up to it."

It was comforting to hear my dad's voice. It reminded me how lucky I was that I wasn't dealing with a family tragedy, but this was also the first time I heard the Grateful Dead referred to in the past tense. He was right that it did really have to end sometime, but what exactly was "it?"

Work was the last place I wanted to be at that moment, so I just left. When I got back to my apartment, I immediately went out on my fire escape with a cold bottle of Rolling Rock. I didn't feel like listening to the Dead's music at that moment, but instead tried to think about why it had meant so much to me. The lyrics never changed even if my interpretations of them did. Songs about life, death, and love that seemed like party anthems years ago held entirely new meanings as I had gotten older. Now I wondered how I'd feel hearing them after today.

It wasn't exactly a shock that Jerry had died, especially from a heart attack in a rehab clinic. He'd been in a diabetic coma in 1986 and if he hadn't recovered I would never have seen him in concert in the first place. The Fall tour of 1992 was even cancelled due to his "exhaustion," caused by years of smoking with no exercise whatsoever.

All of this was underscored by the fact that he'd been using heroin for almost 20 years. By 1995, he looked as heavy as ever but was somehow simultaneously wasting away. He looked like a husk of the person he once was. His hair was stringy and his features looked like they were carved out of old wood. I never thought of the fact that he was dying right in front of me because I didn't want to accept the truth. Clearly, accepting when it was time to let go of something would never be my strong suit.

A half hour later, I was onto my fourth beer. I thought about Jerry's refusal to cancel the Deer Creek show. Not only did he insist on playing the show, but he specifically picked songs that dealt with death. "Dire Wolf," with its chorus of "don't murder me," immediately came to mind. When asked about his deification by millions of fans, he joked, "I'll put up with it until they come at me with the cross and nails." Being Jerry Garcia had clearly taken its toll on him, but he always kept his outlaw spirit and humor. No matter how sloppy the shows got, however, I would never stop attending. His death was the only way Jerry was going to stop. I guess it was the same for me.

I even felt a small sense of relief that Jerry's death forced me into a decision I never would have made on my own. Then I immediately felt guilty as hell for admitting it to myself. I decided to turn on 1010 WINS, New York's all-news radio. I had never listened to it, or any news radio station, but I had a feeling this would be a "developing story."

Of course, it was the first thing I heard when I tuned in. "Legions of faithful devotees known as Deadheads have lost Jerry Garcia, their patriarch, today." Then they played a sound bite of one such female devotee. "Dead shows were a way of life, man. The band and the audience had this connection and that all began with Jerry."

I knew exactly what this girl was trying to say, but felt like she'd just sound like another stoned hippie to everyone listening. I guess it didn't matter anyway because neither of us would be seeing any shows. They always seemed to be the backdrop for so many pivotal moments in my life, but was that just because I was always on tour?

I decided to turn off the radio. Whatever my next move was, I'd be doing it without the security of there being another Dead show. It had gotten to the point that I couldn't tell if they were my vacations from the real world or just attempts to hide from the disappointment I'd felt since graduation.

Somewhere down Third Avenue, I heard someone blasting "I Know You Rider" from *Europe '72*. The news was really starting to spread now. I thought about all the shows where I'd heard this song. Everyone always eagerly anticipated Jerry singing his verse about wishing he was a headlight on a north bound train. It was always a high point, as he often belted it out with his most enthusiastic singing of the night. It was sort of a barometer for how into the show he was. At the show my dad attended, I remember him being amazed at the tidal wave of applause after Jerry sang those words.

He gave it his all the last time I saw him sing those words at Giants Stadium a few months back, but it was clear now that years of hard living were taking their final toll. A rehab counselor from the Haight said it best a few days later in a *San Francisco Chronicle* piece I saw online:

"He appears to have had multiple medical problems that caught up with him. He would have died at Disneyland. He would have died here. He would have died anywhere. He's lucky that he made it this far."

At least he didn't die at Disneyland. I would no longer struggle to balance the two worlds I tried to live in. Maybe this was fate's way of giving me a clean slate for the rest of my "journey."

Rudy Giuliani nixed the proposed memorial in Central Park the following week, but people still showed up. I liked the idea of an outlaw gathering, especially if it was against Giuliani. DJ, Hollywood, and I walked around the park with beers in hand looking for something. We weren't sure what it was and it became clear everybody else was in the same situation. The cops seemed to be focusing only on people openly smoking weed. A few people were selling shirts of Jerry with the years of his birth and death on them. They obviously didn't have much time to print them up and it showed. The pictures on the front were clearly from the last year of his life. They were now too depressing to look at. It felt like that last Delt party we had where we were clearly trying to conjure up something that was already gone.

I asked my friends what plans they had that night.

"There's a fight on. It's Mike Tyson's first one since getting out of prison. Let's get some beers and invite people over," Hollywood replied.

I really needed a distraction from what was traditionally my distraction at that very moment.

"Let's make it a *keg*," I said.

DIAL "0" FOR JOBLESS

I HAD BEEN STANDING in the same place in line for fifteen minutes now without moving an inch. Every now and then, I'd step to the side just to see if I could get a view of the front. No luck. I didn't think it was possible to be slower than the Department of Motor Vehicles, but the unemployment office made it look like the model of efficiency. At least at the DMV, I knew what was at the end of the line.

Since I was so far back, I passed the time looking at the other people waiting. They didn't look at all like what I'd imagined. The women had briefcases and the men had daily planners. These people looked like they actually had somewhere else to be. I, on the other hand, had dressed for what I thought was the part. I wore my dirtiest khakis and my most faded flannel shirt in the hopes that I'd elicit enough sympathy to get some much-needed rent money.

After finally reaching the counter, however, I realized it didn't matter what I looked like. An elderly woman with a permanent scowl fixed under her drug store eyeglasses stared me down as I approached the counter.

"Please state the reason for your visit today."

I wasn't actually entering another country, even though it felt like it.

"Excuse me?"

"What is the reason you want to file for unemployment, sir?"

I thought I would have to make some impassioned plea, but after about twenty seconds of my rambling she pushed a stack of forms across the counter.

"When you're finished, please go and wait in the classroom."

A classroom? I couldn't believe that after two years in the workforce I was not only returning to school but apparently majoring in how to file for unemployment. There was so much paperwork in front of me, though, I didn't have time to consider how I'd ended up here.

After finally finishing the forms, I walked into the room to see metal chairs arranged in front of a chalkboard. After a few minutes, a man in a threadbare gray sweater entered. He didn't seem particularly enthusiastic. He was teaching the unemployment class, after all. After a brief introduction, he wheeled in a VCR hooked up to a television and turned off the lights.

"Hi, I'm Regis Philbin. Welcome to the New York City Department of Labor."

It felt like watching a bit from *The Simpsons*.

"People say I've got a bunch of jobs, but I know what it's like not to have one. There's no greater city than New York but it's a tough town to live in when you're unemployed."

Regis went on to describe many of the forms sitting in front of us. For the first couple of weeks, we'd need to file using the paper coupons provided. After that, however, we could utilize the New York State Department of Labor's "Tel-Service Line."

"It's so simple," Regis said. Now it sounded like he was in a late-night commercial. "You just follow the phone prompts. When asked if you worked the previous week, you just push 1 for 'YES' and 0 for 'NO.' Then do the same in response to the question about your looking for a job to the best of your ability.'"

At the end of the video, our teacher imparted a final warning:

"The last thing I'll remind you of is the most important thing. If you don't file for unemployment by midnight on Sunday, you won't be eligible to claim for that week at all. Also, be sure to keep records of your job search since the Department of Labor will be checking on you."

That didn't surprise me, but I couldn't imagine why we needed such a stern reminder to file for benefits. If you're unemployed wouldn't that be the first thing on your to-do list? I left the unemployment office feeling a little humbled but mostly grateful.

Thanks to all the overtime I was forced to work as a paralegal, my yearly earnings would allow me to claim a weekly benefit of $300. That would be enough to tide me over for a few months, especially since I had moved in with DJ in the East Village.

I had taken Money's old room at 99 Second Avenue, between 5th and 6th Streets. The apartment was essentially one long hallway housed over a deli. There were four rooms, with only the outside two having windows. It wasn't zoned for residential use, but had been rented out for years. Our mailbox was made of cardboard and sat next to the display counter in the deli. When DJ and Money first moved in, they found the entire wardrobe of the previous occupants who were clearly "working girls." Maybe that's why the apartment had been zoned as a "business residence."

My parents knew there was a little shadiness afoot, but were supportive enough to look the other way. They knew I wasn't happy for the last two years and helped cover the security deposit and first month's rent.

It was still early afternoon when I left the Department of Labor, so I decided to walk from West 20th. It would take about a half hour to get home. As I walked, I thought about what I'd do after the unemployment ran out. I could always get a temp job even if it was as a legal assistant. If I knew it was short term, I could endure it. I might be treading water vocationally for a bit, but at least I would be in fresh surroundings. The apartment was only a few blocks from St. Mark's Place and its countless hard-to-find CD shops, T-shirt booths, and independent video stores. CBGB was nearby as was the block from Zeppelin's *Physical Graffiti* album. The Stones even filmed the video for "Waiting On A Friend" there. The coolest thing, though, was that the long-defunct Fillmore East—home to some of the greatest concerts of all time by the Dead, Allmans, Who, and Hendrix to name a few—was next door.

It was now just a vacant space after being a gay nightclub in the 1980s. In the weeks after Jerry's death, it had become a makeshift shrine. When my dad and I unpacked the Ryder truck on the day I moved in, we saw countless roses, beer cans, and candles at the base of the wall that faced Second Avenue. Someone had even wheatpasted an old poster of Jerry from the 1970s up there.

As I walked up the stairs, I wondered if his passing would end up being the thing that helped me finally find myself after graduation. I unlocked the door to the apartment and saw the living room. There were cheeseburger remnants enveloped by crumpled aluminum foil left on the blue plastic table that faced the TV.

Over the couch was a framed reprint of the famous 1983 *New York Post* front page with the "HEADLESS BODY IN TOPLESS BAR" headline. Over the television hung a poster from *True Romance*, with Christian Slater dry humping Patricia Arquette amidst a sea of bullet holes. At least it wasn't from the by-then-clichéd *Reservoir Dogs* or *Pulp Fiction*.

DJ built sets at the Home Shopping Network in Queens. His hours changed weekly, which meant I always had someone to drink with. Without work in the morning, it felt great to go out on a Sunday night for the first time since college. He and Money knew a few East Village bartenders, so we'd often drink for free. More importantly, they let me use the phone at 11:59 when I remembered I had an important call to make.

EBONY & IRONY

FOR THE FIRST TIME SINCE GRADUATION, I was starting to feel good about myself. My life wasn't perfect, but I was enjoying it finally. Money was right; it's all in the way you look at it.

Part of that perspective came from writing again. I began

submitting freelance pieces wherever I could. I wrote a few bits for some books on the Dead. It was great to not only have my name in print but to know that my parents could go to their Barnes and Noble and see it.

Of course, I wasn't yet getting paid for my work. I knew temping after the unemployment ran out would be my last chance to hit pause on finding a career path, so I figured I'd look into sports writing.

I hadn't done it since high school, but it still seemed like the most natural fit. It's what I knew the most about, besides the Dead. I started calling every newspaper in the Tri-state area about openings. Sadly, every conversation seemed to follow the same script:

"What kind of writing experience do you have?"

"Well, I was Sports Editor of my high school news—"

"What about college?"

I certainly couldn't explain my actions during those four years, much less their meaning.

"I mostly concentrated on my studies during college."

"Our entry-level reporters are always recent college graduates with at least five years sports media experience."

"Well, maybe I'll be calling you in five years or so."

I was about to give up when I realized there were two papers I hadn't called. *The City-Sun* and *The Amsterdam News* were New York's two African-American periodicals, both with separate sports sections. At this point, I had nothing to lose and decided to give it a shot. I started with *The City-Sun*. "What kind of opportunities do you have for freelance sportswriters?"

"Well, normally they'd be pretty good, but we have to cut our payroll as it is."

I sensed an opening, even if it was an unpaid one.

"I'd be willing to write for free for a while."

"Send over a resume and some clips and we'll take a look."

A few weeks later, I got a voicemail message:

"I'm looking for Rob Gross. This is Zuri Jelani from *The City-Sun*. I got your clips and would like for you to come down to our offices if you're still interested."

I felt a mixture of excitement and fear on the subway ride down to Brooklyn the following day. I grabbed a copy of their most recent issue at the newsstand before leaving.

The red, black, and green masthead read: *The City-Sun: Speaking Truth To Power*. As if that wasn't intimidating enough, the week's cover story was "Blacks and Jews: Can They Get Along?" I quickly flipped the paper over to the sports section. There were articles on boxing and basketball, but no football. They had to see something in my writing if they wanted to meet me, but I couldn't possibly imagine what it was.

Sitting in their waiting room waiting for the Managing Editor didn't do anything to enlighten me. There were framed posters of some of their biggest stories on the walls. The subjects included The Central Park Jogger, Tawana Brawley, and O.J. Simpson. By this point, I had to find out what made them call me if only to satisfy my own curiosity.

It was only a few minutes before Zuri came to get me. Her braided black hair spilled out from under a patterned silk scarf. If she was shocked by my skin color, she definitely didn't show it.

"I bet you're wondering why we called you in, Rob."

"To be honest . . ."

"That's okay. I'll be straight with you. Our circulation has been down for a while. *The Amsterdam News* doesn't have it quite as bad up there in Harlem. That's because they're soft on any black public figure in their reporting. They're just happy to see any African-American in the spotlight. They've been after us ever since we went after David Dinkins as mayor."

"Okay, Ms. Jelani, but I'm not sure what has to do with me."

"Call me Zuri. Look, Rob, we need to take some chances here. We already have boxing and basketball covered, but it seems like you're interested in football."

"You could say that."

"It also seems like you write in a pretty personal voice. I like that. Our stuff is opinionated, but not when it comes to sports. Feel free to insert some commentary into your articles. You can tell the reader who your favorite team is. I read pieces from your online newsletter. Are you interested in anything besides football?"

"I'm also a Mets fan, although you could argue that means I don't know anything about baseball."

She laughed and told me that was the type of stuff she wanted me to write. True to her word, Zuri published my writing for almost a year after that. As I gained her trust, she even let me cover basketball and boxing when the regular reporters weren't available. The best part was that she let me drop references into my work, no matter how obscure. When asked to write a piece about that week's NFL Action, I sent back an article entitled "In Memory of Andre Reed." I couldn't imagine they'd know that I subbed in the name of a Bills wide receiver into an Allman Brothers instrumental, but they left it in.

After working for free for the first six months, the paper even started paying me for my articles. I had to show up at the offices to receive my check, but that ritual only added to my growing sense of pride. After Zuri signed each voucher, I'd give it to payroll and watch them cut the check for me. After learning that the paper was facing even more financial troubles than when I started, I felt especially honored. When Zuri left me a message one week to hold off faxing her my assignment, I didn't think much of it at first. Soon after, though, she also suggested I stay away from the office until further notice.

I was a little confused until I saw something on TV that weekend. DJ, Money, and I were out at a bar and I saw a graphic that said, "Black Newspaper Owes IRS $380,000" on the screen. I had the bartender turn up the volume and watched as they showed the Brooklyn office with padlocks on it.

"It looks like when they raided Studio 54," Money joked.

"At least the checks cleared," DJ added.

I never told my parents why I stopped writing for the paper, but I did send them a big package of all the issues I appeared in. Their local bookstore didn't yet have a section for "ethnic newspapers" such as the *Jewish Forward*, *El Diario*, or *Irish Echo*. A few months later, however, my dad told me they'd read my articles.

"Once I got your mother to skip past the editorial by the Nation of Islam about the 'Israeli bloodsuckers,' we really enjoyed your writing style."

LIGHTNING BOLT OF INSPIRATION

FREELANCING LIT A SPARK IN ME. Sports, movies, and music were all pretty easy topics for me to opine on. As a result, I couldn't tell how strong my writing actually was. I was walking from the 6 train after a temp job when I spotted a yellow newspaper dispenser on the corner. It read "Gotham Writers Workshop." They had similar boxes all over the city, but I'd never thought to open one up until then. I'd always connected them in my head to seminars of "The Learning Annex," which seemed like an outright scam. With course titles like "Be an Instant Oil Repairman" and "So You Want To Open a Boutique," it was easy to dismiss any catalog left in stacks on the street. I pulled the handle and grabbed one off the top. There were writers' workshops in every conceivable genre, even "Creative Nonfiction." Hunter Thompson once wrote that the best fiction was truer than any kind of journalism. Maybe this class could help me learn to write about things I wasn't a self-proclaimed expert on.

There was a beginners' class with no prerequisite beyond bringing a sample piece to the first class. However, all my freelance pieces were more creative than nonfiction. I decided I'd bring an issue of my Chargers newsletter. I enjoyed writing most when it felt like I was just talking anyway. *Justice Is Coming*, now in its second year of existence, was definitely that.

I was nervous for the first class, especially since I assumed we'd have our work critiqued that night. But the instructor immediately put those fears to rest.

"My name is Max Miller. I have an MFA from Columbia and work as an editor at Wiley and Sons. The goal of this class isn't to belittle and discourage you. The process of trying to get published will do that enough. The course catalog lists the only prerequisite as having written something that you think represents your voice. Before the next class, I'll have a chance to read it and help you to develop that voice."

Of course, I didn't know that Max would photocopy all of our work so that everyone could chime in. We began the second class seated at a long conference table. I immediately flashed back to that first day of kindergarten. At the very least, I was pretty sure I wasn't going to be kicked out and sent home.

Max had an easygoing tone to his voice, which made it a little easier when he asked me to read my piece out loud.

"What I saw out there made me sick, Buttermaker, you know that? I survived the game a week ago in New Jersey just for this team to lose at home in the playoffs? If you saw the newscasts from the Meadowlands Christmas Eve, you know what I'm talking about. Yeah, I heard that story. If those goombahs try any more rough stuff you tell 'em . . . I ain't no bandleader.

Seriously, I survived a game where 175 fans got ejected for throwing snowballs on the field. Every Chargers fan I saw was under attack and I had to watch it all from the upper deck like Edward Murrow if he had a gallon of Bloody Marys in him. Our 60-year old equipment manager got knocked unconscious by one, for God's sake. The Chargers overcame a 17-3 halftime deficit that day for what, exactly? They lost to a Colts team who hadn't won in the postseason SINCE 1971. Humphries throws 4 picks, including one that Tony Martin had in his hands for a touchdown. We give up 147 yards rushing to a guy named Zack Crockett, who does not have a pet alligator named Elvis, by the way. It's hard to believe that anything could wreck New Year's Eve in Manhattan but the Chargers having their season ended on Sunday did it."

Max began by asking the other students what they thought of it. Many of them were women who appeared to be in their late 30s, so I braced myself for the worst. Even if they were football fans, I couldn't expect them to connect to it.

"It was actually pretty funny," one said.

"Yeah, I saw that Giants game on TV. I can't believe you survived that rooting for the other team."

"Was that a reference to *Miami Vice* at the end?"

"Rob," Max said. "There was some *Godfather* and *Bad News Bears* stuff in there as well, am I right?"

"Uh, yeah."

"Were you making all those jokes because your team lost or were you trying to do something else with your writing?"

"I don't know. I think it was more of a way of connecting to the reader and feeling them out."

"How so?"

"I want to make sure they like the same stuff beyond the Chargers. It's kind of like speaking in a code to see if they're cool enough to keep reading."

"Interesting. I don't know if I've seen sports writing like that before. It reminds me a little of Hunter Thompson's style before he got too big with all that Gonzo stuff."

This guy definitely had my attention.

"You know, he wrote a novel in the 1950s. It was titled *Prince Jellyfish*, I believe. He never finished it, but he published the excerpts in one of his books a few years back. You should check that out. I think it might inspire you. But don't give up on the football stuff, since you never know."

I went to The Strand bookstore the next day to pick up a copy of the book, *Songs Of The Doomed*. I couldn't even get out of the store's famous stacks before starting it. Max was right. This was Thompson writing about living in Greenwich Village in the 1950s, meeting girls, and eventually fleeing the city for upstate New York. It almost read like JD Salinger or John Knowles, but had that little hint of menace under the surface. *This* was creative nonfiction. I didn't know if I had a life story interesting enough to tell, but thought I'd give it a shot.

I paid for the book and headed home. As soon as I got there, I turned on my Mac and got started. I thought about growing up in Chappaqua and two words popped into my head:

Suburban Incubation.

WRITE ABOUT THAT

WITH *THE CITY-SUN* CLOSED DOWN, I feared my freelancing days were over. I knew I couldn't temp much longer since my COBRA benefits would soon expire. Even with my parents' help with the prohibitive premiums, the 18-month limit would force me back into a full-time job. For now, however, the satisfaction I was getting from writing offset the mundane work needed to pay bills. My resulting confidence also allowed me to get laid with some regularity for the first time since college. I just had returned from the apartment of a girl I met in a writing class I was taking. when I saw a letter waiting for me at the deli.

It was from *Sports Illustrated*. It was a legal sized envelope, not the small ones from Subscriber Services. I quickly opened it up. I had sent the magazine some clips about six months ago and had long since given up hope. I quickly tore it open.

"Mr. Gross: I am in charge of hiring reporters, the *main*

entry-level position on our editorial staff. We do not have any current openings and very rarely do. Our reporters have one major function, which is to check stories for accuracy. It can be tedious and requires not so much journalistic talent as it does concern, care, and attention to detail. Reporters are willing to wait for several years while waiting to be promoted to a writing or editing position, if indeed that happens."

I began to wonder why they even bothered writing me. The letter went on to explain that the only way I could be considered for a reporter position was to write an "advance text piece," which is essentially a spec article. The letter ended by saying that I could pick the topic of my piece and wished me luck if I chose to submit it to them. It felt like they were daring me to write it.

Maybe I was daring myself. I didn't know how good a writer I was, but I knew this would probably be my best shot to find out. I needed a topic worthy of *Sports Illustrated*, but couldn't think of something to distinguish myself. I was mulling it over with Money and DJ late one night when one of our favorite bartenders mentioned he had a family friend who played linebacker at NC State.

"He's from Jersey and the crazy thing is that he can barely hear."

"He's deaf?" I asked.

"Pretty much. He wears hearing aids, but has to take them off when he puts on his helmet."

The idea of someone playing linebacker in silence sounded like the perfect hook for an article. The bartender agreed to call for me the next day. Fortunately, the linebacker was from New Jersey and was home visiting before having to get back to school. We agreed to meet at one of the eight million Starbucks that had sprung up around the city over the last few years. Rich Strelnick wasn't hard to spot, since he was gigantic. I had never seen a real college football player in person—Division III Rochester guys didn't count. I brought a tape recorder with me even though I wasn't sure how we'd be able to communicate. It turned out that he could hear just fine sitting across from me. The hearing aids he'd used in both ears since he was eight were incredibly effective even though they also amplified all the surrounding noise as well.

"Makes it tough to talk to girls at parties," he joked.

This was my first real interview, but Rich made it easy. He detailed the fear and helplessness that came from having his hearing gradually disappear beginning at age five. He described his frustration and subsequent aggression at being seen as stupid when he simply couldn't understand the people talking to him. That had led to a lot of self-medicating,

"It was a lot easier just to drink instead of deal with people at bars. You know what I mean?"

"I actually do," I said.

It turned out that Rich had lost two years of eligibility due to alcohol-fueled fights. He spent a year at home seeing psychologists rather than AA counselors.

"Drinking was the symptom, but not the problem."

After talking to him for an hour, I knew I had enough for the piece. I just needed to write better than I ever had in order to do his story justice. Fortunately, my writing instructor encouraged us to bring in new material for the class to critique. It took almost a month to finish, but I finally did it. I felt really good afterwards, even if I didn't expect to hear back from *Sports Illustrated*.

Instead of another letter, I got a phone call a month later.

"Mr. Gross, we received your advance text piece. There are no openings for reporters currently, as we outlined in our letter. However, we were impressed enough with the article that we would like to purchase its rights. Please get back to us if that arrangement works for you."

I couldn't believe it. I immediately called back, not quite believing the message. Diana, one of the managing editors, confirmed that I would receive $700 for the piece. This was more than I had gotten for all of my previous writing combined. She told me I could come up to the Time-Life building and pick up my check.

I printed out a copy of the article to take on the subway ride up to Rockefeller Plaza. I still couldn't believe that they wanted to buy it and wanted to look it over once last time.

When I got there, I expected to be shuttled right to payroll. However, this was nothing like *The City-Sun*. The receptionist told me I could wait until Diana was available. I was still in shock. This was *Sports Illustrated*. Steinbeck, Kerouac, and Faulkner had all written for them. Even Hunter Thompson took his assignment to cover the Mint 400 motorcycle race and turned it into *Fear and Loathing in Las Vegas*. While I waited, I read my article to calm my nerves:

Silent Ovation, by Rob Gross

"From his middle linebacker perch, Rich Strelnick locks the Seminole quarterback into the crosshairs. It is top-ranked Florida State's 1995 home opener and the fans are even more raucous than usual. Thousands of flailing arms cut through the Tallahassee sunlight as the 'Tomahawk Chop' battle cry engulfs the stadium. But for Strelnick the only crowd noise he feels are the vibrations under his feet."

Not fucking bad, I had to admit. After a few minutes, Diana came out to meet me. Her office was filled with books that were all written or edited by someone who worked at the magazine. If I wasn't already aware that I was inside one of the most respected sports publications on earth, I sure was now.

"This was very well-written, Rob. We don't often buy freelance pieces, but your article showed a lot of promise."

"It did?"

"It's raw, obviously. But it was clear from the quotes you used that your interview techniques were effective." She read off a few examples:

"'When people run, I run. When they stop, I stop. You can hear everyone in the world talking to you and it still won't sink in.' The words bring the reader in without losing them. You also used

good anecdotes, like the one about opposing players trying to intimidate him by making faces at him."

"Thanks so much," I effused. "I can't believe I'm going to be in *Sports Illustrated.*"

"Rob, I don't think you understand. We're buying your piece, but that doesn't mean we're publishing it."

My heart dropped. I couldn't believe what I was hearing.

"We're purchasing the piece from you and if the subject goes on to do something in the NFL we *might* publish it."

She could sense my disappointment.

"Don't be discouraged. You clearly like to write about things that interest you. I read your other clips. It seems like you are quite a Chargers supporter."

I chuckled to myself. "That's one way to put it."

"I used to be a big Boston Red Sox fan. But writing full-time means you wouldn't be able to remain a 'fanatic,' so to speak."

"Why is that?"

"When you are covering the game, you don't care who wins or loses. You just want to be sure to make your deadline. It also seems like you have a lot of interests outside of sports."

"I guess I like to drop in references to music, movies, and television because it's a way to connect to other people who like same stuff. It's like a secret handshake or password that you've found someone who 'gets it.' It's like what the guys on *Sports Center* are starting to do."

"I know they're trying to reach out to a younger audience, but I wonder if that's just a fad. It sounds like the kind of 'alternative journalism' you're describing might work on the internet. I'm going to give your name to our new web publishing group. They're just getting off the ground, but you should look to see what other publications are moving on-line."

Sure, I wished I had used my hunch to create one of the many sports/pop culture blogs that exist today. But at least I walked out the Time-Life building knowing I could sell my work and that maybe there would be other outlets willing to buy it. Diana was right. I could never abandon being a fan in favor of becoming an objective reporter. However, there were several magazines looking to "go alternative," on the page and on the internet. I was even able to write for a few of them in the years to come. At that moment, however, I just needed was something to pay the bills that I could tolerate doing every day.

I CALL MYSELF THE TEACHER?

"YOU MIGHT ACTUALLY BE pretty good at it," Money said.

"Teaching? You mean like for a *job*?"

"Yeah. I never mentioned it before, but my mom works in the personnel department of one the school districts in Brooklyn. They're always looking for new teachers."

Even with a degree in history, I had never considered going into education. I had trouble accepting a position of responsibility in the fraternity, let alone with a room full of students. Plus, there was nothing less outlaw than being a teacher.

"Think about it, Luca. Just don't try to be the kids' friend. My mom says that's where new teachers get chewed up."

"I didn't take any teaching classes at Rochester, though. How would I even get a license?"

"That's just it," he said. "You would be pretty close to getting certified in social studies. Didn't you major in history? All you'd have to do is take some education classes at night to get certified."

I liked history, but couldn't imagine getting kids to learn it. However, I didn't have any other options at this point. I couldn't push the snooze button on getting a full-time job anymore. My parents had stretched themselves pretty thin financially after helping with the medical plan and writing classes.

It took an entire day at the Board of Education in Brooklyn to get a temporary teaching certificate. I was fingerprinted, but still would have to wait to pass a background check. I also filled out a ton of applications, ordered duplicate transcripts, and agreed to take some teaching tests. If I wanted to get a permanent license, I'd have to eventually get a Master's Degree.

While I rode the subway back to the East Village, I looked at the stack of papers in my lap.

Rob Gross: Secondary Social Studies 7-12.

I still couldn't wrap my head around it. As a student myself, I thought of teachers only as obstacles I had to get around. Now I was going to be one of them?

But Money was right. There was so much turnover in New York City teaching at the time that they were more than willing to give me a shot. After it was confirmed that I had no existing police record, I was assigned to a junior high school in the Williamsburg section of Brooklyn.

This was before the neighborhood was gentrified into the hipster haven it is today. Money told me the neighborhood was divided between the Hasidic Jews who went to private yeshivas and the predominantly Hispanic population that attended public school.

I was replacing a teacher who was about to retire. Before my first day, I came in to meet with him after the kids had left for the day. He looked like the spitting image of Danny DeVito and was fast sleep at his desk. His grey slacks, right out of the 1973 Sears catalog, were pulled so high over his bulging stomach that he could have unzipped them and left a V-Neck collar around his neck. How was I going to replace this guy?

After waking him up, he attempted to advise me. "So, you want to be a teacher?"

"I'm not really sure. I haven't really had any preparation."

"That shit doesn't matter. All you need to do is to stay a day ahead of the kids. The biggest mistake kids make when they start teaching is they're afraid to put down their script."

"You mean like a lesson plan?"

"Yeah. No matter how well you plan, you're gonna have to improvise. It's like how those jazz guys would start and finish with the same song, but in the middle they'd be winging it."

Okay, so like a good solo, I thought to myself. That I could definitely relate to.

"Remember what Mike Tyson said before the Holyfield fight? Everybody's got a plan until they get punched in the mouth."

"But didn't Tyson lose that fight after biting Holyfield's ear off?"

"That's not the point," he said. "You'll see."

On the way to school that first Monday, I thought about how I would start the class. I had a lesson planned on the Reconstruction period all ready to go. I had an arsenal of notes, readings, and activities that I knew I might need to deviate from. I just needed a way to break the ice with the kids. I assumed opening with "Aloha, my name is Mr. Hand" from *Fast Times at Ridgemont High* would go right over their heads. As the kids took their seats, I could sense their anticipation. They were feeling me out. I had already written my name and the aim of the lesson on the blackboard and figured someone in the class would know what the word *reconstruction* meant. That would hopefully be a nice segue into the introductory activity. The kids were way more developed physically than the ones I went to middle school with. With a student body that was ninety-five percent Dominican and Puerto Rican, I saw more than a few gold doorknocker earrings and shining crucifixes. Before I could even open my mouth, one of the boys in the front row spoke up.

"Hold up. Mr. *Gross*? What kind of a name is that?"

He was over six feet tall with a Caesar-style haircut and a red, white, and blue Tommy Hilfiger polo shirt buttoned to the top.

I was about to tell him to raise his hand when I decided to just answer the question.

"I'm not sure what you mean," I said. "It's just my last name and I'm not really sure what it has to do with anything. What's your name?"

"It's Marco. Look we're Spanish, right?"

"It would appear so," I responded a little too dryly.

"*Oooooooohhhhhhhh*," the class moaned.

"Yo, Mr. G. Are you trying to diss me?"

I had to cut this off. "Not at all, Marco. I guess I just don't understand what you're asking, that's all."

"We're Spanish. Some teachers are Irish and this country used to be all British. So what are *you*?"

"What am I? Like what 'ish' am I?"

The class laughed.

"I'm just white and Jewish."

"You're Jewish?" At this point every kid in the class was glued to our exchange.

"Yes, Marco. I thought the wavy hair and the sarcasm would have tipped you off."

Silence.

"Yeah, but you don't have the black hat or coat. You definitely don't have those curly sideburns."

It took me about ten minutes to explain the difference between me and the men they saw on Marcy Avenue every day. As I spoke, other kids started raising their hands and asking questions. It was obvious that they had never met a non-Orthodox Jew, or at least weren't aware that they had. I answered each question while maintaining my composure, even when they asked me if I had sex through a sheet.

I looked at the clock and realized that I only had ten minutes left in the period.

"Okay, you guys started talking about Reconstruction on Friday, right?"

Patty, a girl in the back of the room, volunteered.

"I don't get why the North didn't just punish the South after the war. Everybody says Lincoln freed the slaves, but when he had a chance to make them pay for starting everything he didn't do it."

"I think you mean his strategy of letting Southern states get back into the Union?"

"I guess . . ."

I had to think fast. "Patty, you ever get in trouble with your mom?"

The class laughed.

"Yeah, definitely."

"If your mom doesn't do anything to you when you mess up, you probably do it again, but what if she punishes you *too harshly*? Are you going to learn whatever it is she's trying to teach you?"

"No, probably not. I think I get what you're trying to say."

Before I could respond, the bell rang. The kids smiled at me as they got up to leave. I didn't get through all the stuff I had planned, but I could pick it up with them tomorrow.

Plus, I had four more classes to teach that day.

I KNEW RIGHT AWAY

WITH A FULL-TIME JOB I DIDN'T HATE, I could finally embrace life after college. Even with the education classes I took at night, I still had time to write. Between teaching and freelancing, I had found a balance between being fulfilled and financially independent. Before I knew it, I was able to afford my own apartment, a studio on East 5th Street and Avenue A. I finished my education classes and started working towards a Master's Degree in history at Hunter College. This put me back in the Upper East Side a couple nights a week, but I felt like a different person now. I finally had shit figured out.

I still partied, but started working out a little too. I lost some weight and gained even more confidence with women. Money and DJ even noticed the difference.

"Thank God, Luca. You were getting really mopey there for a while."

We were walking up Second Avenue after a Saturday night showing of *Deuce Bigalow: Male Gigolo*. We'd split a twelve pack in the theater and were looking for some trouble to get into.

"Shit, Money. Tell me how you really feel."

"You know what he's saying," DJ added. "We were still doing all the same stuff we did in college, but it seemed like sometimes you forgot how to enjoy it."

"You mean like I was just going through the motions?"

"Bet," Money said. "I hooked you up with the teaching gig and look how happy you are. Also, what did I tell you about girls? If you give off a positive vibe, they can sense that."

We decided to hit a bar. Luckily, I remembered McSwiggan's was nearby. I hadn't been there since Money conducted his one-man intervention on me.

The place was packed and it didn't take long to realize that someone was having a party. It was December 11th, still a little early for a holiday celebration. Yet there was a line of girls at the bar doing shots. A few of them seemed to have boyfriends standing behind them, but everyone was all focused on the brunette at the center of the bar. She was wearing a black tank top with orange flames in the center and black leather pants. She may have been dressed like all my rock-star fantasies come to life, but something about her also looked familiar. As the bar screamed "HAPPY 25th!" I realized she'd been in one of my classes at Hunter. I told Money and DJ.

"You should buy her a drink," said DJ.

"I agree. It's clearly her birthday. It would almost be rude not to," Money joked.

I'd never approached a girl like this before and had no idea it would be my one and only time. The Stones "Midnight Rambler" was blaring so loudly from the jukebox that I almost had to shout to get her attention. When I tapped her on the shoulder, she turned her head around. Her sweet smile gave me the last-second boost of confidence to introduce myself.

"I think . . . uh, I took a class at Hunter with you."

"You did?"

Sammy would later tell me that while she didn't remember me from class, she was impressed with my assertiveness. She also didn't want to admit that she'd dropped the class, although I didn't blame her. It was really boring.

"It was that Western Civilization course where the professor just read his handwritten notes for two hours straight without taking a breath," I told her.

"I hated that class," she said.

"I don't blame you. That guy was a dick."

She laughed. "I love your shirt."

I was wearing an old shirt with the cover photo to Springsteen's *Darkness on the Edge Of Town* on it."Thanks," I said. "Most people don't notice it."

"How is that even possible? I mean it's *Bruce*."

"You've seen him in concert?"

"Are you kidding? My brother took me to my first show at the Garden in 1988. It was the *Tunnel of Love* tour and was totally amazing. It's one of those things you can't describe unless you experience it. It's actually hard to explain."

"Actually, you did a pretty good job." The way her face lit up while discussing the Boss drew me in, but I was also a little scared at how attractive I found it. "I'm Rob, by the way."

She grabbed my hand. "Nice to meet you Rob. I'm Samantha—Sam."

"So what have you been up to since Hunter College, Sam?"

"I've been temping while I try to figure out what I want to do. It's kind of scary being out of college. I'm thinking about becoming a school social worker."

I looked behind me to see Money and DJ nod in approval.

"It's your birthday. Let me buy you a shot. What'll you have?"

"Chilled Southern Comfort. What do *you* do, Rob?"

"I've been teaching middle school social studies."

"Thanks for the shot, but now you've gotta get me a fucking job!"

I had to find out a little more about this girl.

Her friends started coming over to check on her, so I figured I should go sit with Money and DJ for a bit. Before I knew it, she was introducing me to everyone.

"This is Rob. We took a class together. Now he's getting me a job."

As unexpected as this all was, it somehow felt natural. Each person I spoke to treated me like I'd known her for a long time. It kind of felt like I did. When Money and DJ got up to leave, they assured me that I should stick around.

"I'm definitely not going anywhere," I happily said.

It was almost 3:00 AM when she grabbed my hand. Appropriately, the Dead's "Friend of the Devil" came on the jukebox. "*This* is the kind of Grateful Dead I like," Sam said. "I don't need a song that goes on forever. No one needs a drum solo, either."

I was about to say something, but stopped myself. I figured I'd reveal my musical allegiances another time. I wasn't being cocky, but somehow seemed sure we'd see each other again. When the bartender announced last call, though, I didn't want the night to end.

I started walking her back to her apartment a few blocks away when we started kissing. I wasn't worried about whether we'd end up in bed together, however. Actually, I wasn't worried about *anything*. When we got to her stoop, it felt like we were two longtime friends who were hesitant to take things to the next level for all the right reasons. We sat down on the concrete ledge.

"We should definitely get together again," I said.

"You mean you'll call?"

"How could I not?"

We started kissing again and I told her I was going to catch a cab. I could tell she was relieved, and I wasn't insulted one bit.

"I'm actually supposed to get up in a few hours," she said.

"You are?"

"Yeah, all my friends are going to the Jets game. You like football, Rob?"

It occurred to me at that moment that the Chargers were playing the Seahawks that day. I hadn't thought about it once.

This was fucking serious.

TAKE ROOT IN THE EARTH, BUT KEEP A PLACE IN THE STARS

WE MET FOR DINNER the following weekend at a nice Italian restaurant in the East Village. As I sat waiting for Sammy at the bar, I suddenly felt a sense of panic. Could Saturday night have been too good to be true? I decided I was getting ahead of myself once again as I sipped my Maker's Mark bourbon.

I could tell something was different, however, as soon as she walked into the restaurant. She still looked cute in her gray sweater and jeans, but seemed a little awkward. She kissed me on the cheek and sat down.

"Told you I'd call," I joked.

"Yeah, I know."

"I guess you never met your friends for that game, huh."

"Yeah, remember how I told you my parents were also coming

into the city for my birthday? I was so hungover that I kept running to the bathroom of the restaurant to throw up."

I was about to laugh, but she didn't look like she was in the mood. Now I was really starting to worry that our first meeting was a mirage. I tried to make some small talk and asked her about her life before coming to the New York City. She told me she grew up in Suffolk County on Long Island, but not much else. I anxiously flashed back to some of those awkward meals with Kerry before we broke up.

The rest of the date went well enough, but she was barely talking. This was causing me to talk even more than usual, which was saying something. For dessert, we ordered S'mores that were cooked tableside. Maybe she knew some of the guys from Camp Birchwood I knew who were also from her hometown of Dix Hills. That could be a conversation starter. Even as chocolate and marshmallows were melted right before us, something still seemed off. The conversation was fine, but it was as if we had taken a step back. She was nursing her wine, which was understandable after our first meeting. However, she was holding back beyond just moderating her drinking.

I wasn't going to be the guy who asks what's wrong on the first date, but had to try something.

"My apartment is only a few blocks from here. We don't even need to go upstairs, but I did see the stoop of your place. It's really the least I can do."

With that, she laughed. We walked over to my apartment where, to my surprise, she agreed to come upstairs. I figured I needed to warn her before letting her inside.

"You have to remember this is the first time I've lived by myself. It might get a little scary in there."

"Now I'm intrigued." She was definitely loosening up now.

She walked in and came face to face with my giant bookshelf of VHS tapes. There were cassettes of all my favorite movies. I bought some used at Tower Records and recorded the rest off cable. Of course, she immediately spotted the most random entry in my collection.

"You have *Fraternity Vacation*? I haven't seen that since it was on HBO all the time as a kid! You know Tim Robbins was in it."

I was about to point that out before she beat me to it.

She looked around at my *Godfather, Animal House*, Grateful Dead, and Chargers posters as she sat on my plastic wicker love seat. She was now smiling.

"This place is great. Why didn't you mention you were such a big football fan? I may have been drunk, but I *know* you didn't say anything about being a Deadhead."

"I'm not sure," I said. "We had such a great night that I didn't want to talk about anything that might seem lame to you."

She squinted as she smiled to indicate she understood.

"Yeah, I guess that's why I was so quiet at dinner. I haven't really dated much and we got along so well when we first met. It scared me a little, to be honest. I thought you might not find me as impressive on a normal date."

"I'm pretty impressed with you right now."

Before I knew it, we were kissing again.

There was no real attempt from either of us to push things further. It wasn't as if I didn't want to sleep with her. On the contrary, it felt like for the first time since Kerry, sex would mean *something*. I wasn't afraid to find out how much, but I wanted to wait until it felt absolutely right. I got the sense that Sam felt the same way.

I began wooing her. During my winter break, I invited her on a day date to the Museum of Natural History. I was thinking of taking my students there and wanted to check out the exhibits beforehand. On the way to the subway, I stopped at a CVS to get her a birthday card. Even if it was a few weeks late, I thought she might appreciate the gesture. I didn't want to come on too strong. I had to make it romantic but still cool. As I sat on the F train, I tried to come up with something to write on it. Then I remembered an offhand comment she made at the bar that first night. I knew exactly what to say.

When I got off the train, I immediately handed it to her. She was clearly surprised and I urged her to open it up.

To The Girl Who Usually Likes Long-Haired Southern-Looking Guys,

Happy Birthday From A Short-Haired Jewish Guy.

Better Luck Next Year,
Rob

She may have only said "thanks," but the look on her face revealed she was feeling a lot more. Her mouth almost looked like Charles Schulz had drawn it, where she was smiling as much as possible before it became a grimace. As we got in line for the museum, I knew I felt just as happy. More importantly, I felt comfortable. It felt different than it had with Kerry. Life was so much more real now and so were my feelings for Sam.

After we left the museum, it was still only 3:00 PM. When Sammy asked what we should do next, my answer came out of my mouth without thinking.

"You wanna meet my dad?"

"Are you serious? That's a pretty big deal, don't you think?"

"He's consulting at a law firm around here and I promised I'd stop by during my vacation. We don't have to if you're not up to it. It'll be like that scene in *Rushmore* where Max Fischer brings Margret Yang to meet his father at his barber shop."

I'd clearly dropped the Wes Anderson reference to impress and relax her. Introducing her to my dad also didn't seem like that big a deal, and that's what frightened me. When my dad met us at the elevator bank, it was clear that he felt at ease with her as well.

The remains of his graying hair needed a trim which made

him look like a mustached version of Larry Fine of the Three Stooges in a suit.

"Boychik!" The expression on my face revealed my embarrassment.

"Hey, Dad . . ."

"Is this one Jewish? Then she'll understand it's a term of endearment."

My dad had no idea I was stopping by, let alone that I was bringing a girl. I assumed that his allusion "this one's" Judaism was a reference to Kerry. Coming by was unplanned, by now that we were here, I really wanted to make a good impression on Sam.

She extended her hand to my dad. "Mr. Gross, it's nice to meet you. I'm Samantha."

Before she could say any more, my dad had her wrapped in a bear hug.

"Come here. Any friend of Robbie's . . ."

My dad was the only person who ever called me that. I looked at Sam, who didn't seem to mind the moment one bit. My dad brought us to his temporary office, where we sat across from his desk.

I turned to Sam. "This feels like the parents meeting with the principal in every movie or TV show in existence."

She laughed. "Is it actually like that in school these days?"

"I've never sat in on a parent meeting at work but I assume not in the fucking slightest."

"Whoa," my dad said. "I see we're pretty comfortable with each other already!"

"Yeah, I guess we are."

"Samantha, did Rob tell you how his mother and I used to take him out to dinner with us? We used to love this seafood place in Connecticut and would put his baby seat right on the table. They didn't even have tablecloths in the place, just newspaper. At first he'd get startled when we started using the mallets on the crabs, but after a while he just laughed. We spilled more than a few drinks on him. Maybe that's where he got his sense of humor."

"Or at least my love of alcohol," I said.

We only spent a few more minutes with my dad before he had to get on a conference call, but I knew he approved of Sam. Once we got into the elevator, she grabbed my hand.

"That was so cool. Thanks for bringing me."

Now I was the one with the Charlie Brown smile. For once, I didn't have the words to describe what I was feeling. When we went back to my apartment, I think we both knew we would sleep together that night. The sex just felt *right*. It felt hot and warm at the same time, like something I couldn't ever see myself without. The best part was that I didn't feel like I had to explain it to Sam because I knew she was feeling it too. We were falling in love with each other.

We were lying in my bed listening to a Bob Dylan bootleg (New Orleans, 5/3/76) while the NFL playoffs were on one Sunday were on when we finally said the words. The Chargers had once again missed the postseason and Vikings were hosting the Cowboys. Sammy had her head on my shoulder while I watched the game.

"I forget sometimes how much fun watching football can be when you don't really care who wins."

She looked up at me as Dylan's voice cracked and creaked through "Love Minus Zero/No Limit."

"I like this song," she said.

I had had the tape since Camp Birchwood and was about to tell her about the specifics of the show and the version when I looked into her eyes.

"You don't want to hear about the bootleg, do you?"

"Nope. But it makes me happy that you want to tell me."

"You know I'm in love with you, right?"

"Right there with you, *Robbie*." As she burst out laughing, I leaned down to kiss her.

FUCK THE FEAR

A FEW WEEKS LATER, I met Sam's parents. She picked a nice restaurant in Gramercy, not far from her place. However, she didn't give me much preparation.

"You'll love 'em. They grew up in Queens, moved to Long Island, and winter in Boca. It's like the Jewish triathlon."

"Okay," I laughed, "do they have any hobbies?"

"Well, they like Las Vegas, which I know doesn't exactly debunk any stereotypes."

The first thing I noticed about Sam's dad when he walked into the restaurant was that he looked a lot like Gene Rayburn from *Match Game PM*. He quickly extended his hand to me as I introduced myself. Her mom had brown hair like Sam but shorter like so many moms seemed to have. As we waited for our drinks to arrive, her dad tried break the ice. Sam had already told them about the teaching and freelancing.

"So, Rob what do you like outside of work? Do you like football? Jets or Giants?"

"Well, I'm actually a Chargers fan."

"Yeah but they play in San Diego. What's your second favorite team?"

"I don't really *do* second favorites, Sir."

Sam kicked me under the table, but I wasn't trying to be a wise ass for once. Wasn't being so loyal a good thing, especially since I was in a relationship with their daughter? After we ordered our dinner, I thought about bringing up music. But the Grateful Dead would conjure up so many stereotypes I'd have to debunk. It was at that moment I heard Frank Sinatra singing "Come Fly with Me" from the bar.

"Gotta love The Chairman," I mumbled.

Sam's parents suddenly looked at each other. "You like Frank Sinatra?"

"Yeah. I actually saw him twice in concert."

Sam looked at me with a look of surprise as well.

"You never told me that."

I gave my best Boon impression as I said, "I've done a lot of things you don't know about."

"I don't think my parents understand the *Animal House* impression, Rob."

"Well, I saw him in Rochester with my roommate but also at Radio City with Don Rickles opening."

"That's great," said Sam's mom. "We saw him a bunch in the '70s and '80s."

"Yeah, Rob. I'm impressed," Sammy said.

Suddenly, the conversation and the alcohol both flowed. Sam's parents asked me to call them "Ken" and "Rita" and her dad told me stories about her childhood. I could tell that both her and her mom had heard them a million times before, but I found it so sweet that both they acted otherwise.

"Rita and I used to have a boat on Kismet in Fire Island. We'd drink, smoke cigarettes, and have a party every night with our friends. Sam, who her mother named after the girl on *Bewitched*, by the way, would sleep down below. Sure enough, we had such a good time one night that we left the hatch open. It must have rained after we passed out and Sam woke up with the floor soaked all around her. She turned out alright, don't you think?"

"Ken, I think she turned out more than alright."

Things between Sammy and I kept running smoothly during those first six months. If anything, maybe they ran too smoothly since I hadn't found any reason *not* to be with her. Without my knowing it, this was my biggest fear of all. Still, I was doing a pretty good job of keeping my obsessive brain at bay with each anxiety-producing milestone we reached. That all changed, though, the day she asked for a key to my apartment.

By this point, we were spending most nights together. She was still temping, but was about to start back at Hunter at night to get her social work degree. On the nights we met at her place, the doorman could always let me in to wait for her. When we met at my place, however, there was no such option. She was sitting on my bed when the subject first came up.

"Rob, it's just a key. I'm three and a half years younger than you and I understand that. What's the problem?"

"Well actually, it's two keys. Remember that I'm between Avenue A and B and need the extra layer of security."

"Very funny. I don't see why it's such a big deal."

I felt inside my pocket for those two Medeco keys and knew she was right. That didn't make it any less frightening, though. I felt anxious, but couldn't figure out exactly why. It was as if all my fears about commitment were behind another dam that was about to break.

"I don't know, Sammy. I'm just scared."

"Change isn't easy. I understand. You're my first real boyfriend. But you have to get past it."

I tried in vain to explain my position. "It's like how I always want to sit on the end of the aisle at the movies just in case I have to go to bathroom. I don't always have to go, but need to know that I can."

"Jesus, Rob! Thank God I didn't suggest we move in together or something. You're acting like it's *me* you're afraid of. How about you think before you speak, Mr. Wordsmith? I think I need some space right now." With that, she stormed out.

I knew it wasn't Sam I was afraid of. It was all that she represented. At least I was smart enough not to say that out loud.

"OWWWWWW!"

The sound came from the stairwell outside the apartment. Sam had left the door open on her way out. I ran down the marble stairs to see her sitting two floors below. She had a look of childish embarrassment on her face that was impossible to resist.

"I fell on my ass," she confessed.

"Where did you think you were going anyway?"

"I don't know. But you've gotta control your fear. It will screw up everything if you let it."

I knew she was right. I knew that the initial intensity of our first few months wouldn't be enough to sustain the relationship. This was the stage where I stopped really trying with Kerry. I didn't have any of the anxiety I felt with Sam because I knew I was in the real world now. This was the girl I wanted by my side for all the everyday stuff and that's what scared me. I'd need to put in the effort to make sure I understood where the fear was coming from. Otherwise, I'd fuck up the best thing I'd ever found.

"I guess I've never been with anyone during all the boring parts of my life. You know, the everyday stuff."

"Rob, I think that's what life is. It can't always be big nights out, games, or concerts. You think we're going to have some life-altering date every night? That stuff doesn't last, or so I've heard."

For a girl who hadn't had a serious boyfriend, she was pretty insightful.

"I guess giving you a key just set off a lot of my fears."

"I love you, but those fears are going to push me away if you let them. I love music, movies, and TV too. But we're not living in a song or script. You've gotta say *fuck the fear.*"

"Fuck the fear? That's got a nice ring to it."

"I'm being serious, Rob. You have to decide for yourself whether you care more about being scared than you care about the effect that fear has on me. By the way, me having a set of keys doesn't mean I'm going to be hanging out in your apartment without you. After today, I'm not even sure I can deal with five flights of stairs."

With that, we were headed to the locksmith.

NOT SURE I WANT THIS

THE ENVELOPE WAS SITTING on the fake brick ledge next to the plants that I never saw anyone water. A year had passed since I had given Sammy those keys and now we really did live together. Our apartment didn't have a doorman, which was why the envelope sat there for three days before I spotted it. "ROB GROSS" appeared under both the National Football League and Chargers' logo. I pulled open the cardboard sleeve, I noticed that there was also a Visa logo on it. I wondered for a moment if they were finally taking official action on my card's continually growing balance. When I read "CONGRATULATIONS," I then wondered whether my spending had earned me an application for an upgraded account. "Mr. Gross, Visa is proud to welcome you to the 2001 class of the Hall of Fans. Due to your continued support of your chosen team, you have been selected to represent them in an exhibit at the Pro Football Hall of Fame in Canton, OH. Please return the enclosed paperwork by the deadline and we will begin the official enshrinement process."

I felt confused, excited, and anxious all at once. First off, I wasn't even sure I entered such a contest. Every so often, I'd see some "Fan of the Year" promotion and send something in. However, I never expected to win since I didn't have a "stadium persona," paint my face, or even root for my hometown team. Then I remembered that I did send in an essay with an attached photo of me at the Super Bowl before the face paint started melting. I wrote about how I had lived in New York all my life, yet never missed a game. I mentioned my first-person Chargers newsletter, now classified as a "blog." Still, "Fan of the Year" and enshrinement in the actual Pro Football Hall of Fame? I still couldn't believe it.

I had no idea how long the envelope had been sitting in the

lobby, so I was shocked to see that the deadline to respond was the following day. I called the woman in charge of the promotion and assured her I'd overnight the forms. While I had her on the line, I had to ask:

"How did I win this?"

"To be honest, sir, we didn't get very many entries from San Diego Chargers fans. As you mentioned that you've always lived in New York, I'm sure that also had something to do with it."

I didn't care if I hadn't emerged from a crowded field. After talking to the Visa representative, I was told that I would be awarded a plaque at an on-field ceremony before a Chargers home game. A duplicate plaque would be placed in the Hall of Fame the following year. The only catch was that I would have to fund my way to San Diego. At least Visa agreed to comp me game tickets since I was the only winner who had to travel such a long distance to accept their award.

When Sam got home from her social work internship in Queens, I told her the big news.

"We don't exactly have the money to book a flight to San Diego, Rob. When would we have to fly out?"

"They told me I could pick the game since I was the only fan who didn't live in his team's home market."

"That's not surprising," she joked.

"Maybe we'll shoot for the game on December 30. At least we'll be back for New Year's in the city. Of course, the Chargers will also probably be out of playoff contention by then."

"Rob, focus. If you want to do this, you have to find a way to make it work financially."

While researching discount flights, I discovered that there actually was a company called "Cheap Tickets." In the days before they were bought out by Orbitz, they had a New York location that functioned like an old-school travel agency.

It only took a minute of sitting in the waiting room for me to start having flashbacks of my days in the unemployment office.

The place was overflowing with people, many of whom looked like they desperately needed sleep. There were others that looked like they were trying to book passage back to their homeland, wherever that might be. The room felt like a pit of desperation and while I was sure no one else was in my specific situation, I was definitely desperate.

After waiting for over an hour, I was able to meet with an agent. The fact that the game was so close to New Year's made tickets to San Diego super exorbitant.

"I could, however, book you a flight to Los Angeles and you could rent a car. We could even get you a discounted hotel in San Diego. The Gaslight District is lovely this time of year."

I was going to need something to bolster my case with Sam.

"I'll take it."

I felt like things were falling into place that morning as we approached the airline counter. I knew we were extending ourselves a little financially, but it was worth it. I couldn't believe Sammy let me find a way to make it work. As I reached inside the backpack for the airline tickets, I wondered what that happiness might mean. We'd been together for two years now. We lived together and clearly our finances were irrevocably intertwined. Was it time to think about marriage?

My anxiety was replaced by full-blown panic when I reached into my backpack and only felt one ticket. I tried not to worry Sam when I flatly asked her if there was a ticket in her pocketbook.

"Rob, *tell me* you didn't leave it in the apartment."

I couldn't believe how stupid I was. I had spent all this money for an opportunity that wouldn't come again. I felt my chest tighten up. The flight was set to leave in thirty minutes. Was I going to miss my shot to be recognized for all those years spent following this maddening football team? Then again, we *did* have one ticket . . .

I put that thought out of my mind as quickly as it had snuck in. There was no way I was going to LA without Sam. However, she knew me well enough to know what I was thinking.

"Rob, you should go. It's *your* award, after all."

There was something about the way she said "your award" that gave me pause. What was I really being honored for? Before we met, I watched every game without a second thought. If the Chargers lost (as they often did), it felt like my whole week had been spoiled. But that had changed since I met Sam. I didn't feel like every week meant so much and I had even missed a game here and there. They had been for the Jewish High Holidays and her brother's wedding in Florida, but that wasn't the point. Although I did have to ask her who would have a wedding that required me to be flying during a game.

"I don't know, Rob. *Society?*"

As I looked into her eyes, I felt like this award was less about the 23 years of fanaticism that had preceded her and more about her putting up with my need to keep it up. There was no way I was making this trip without her.

"There's no point in going without you."

"But we can't afford another ticket. It was a stretch to buy this one."

The woman behind the counter had obviously heard our conversation because she politely suggested that we buy an additional seat for the flight.

"They clearly only gave you a single seat. Why else would you bring just one to the airport? How did you purchase the tickets?"

"With a Visa card," I replied.

"I'm sure you could file a claim for the *missing* ticket."

Even though what she was suggesting wasn't guaranteed to work, it was our only chance right now. I wasn't worried about deceiving Visa, unless it meant they'd strip me of my award.

Our flight and drive went smoothly and we were able to even to enjoy a night out in the Gaslight District of San Diego. When we arrived at the stadium the following morning, we were led through the media entrance. From there, we were directed to the tunnel where I'd seen the players emerge from since I was a kid. There were painted helmets of every team, with the Chargers at the very end. We walked through the makeshift gazebo, which dumped us out onto the field. Waiting for us was the representative from Visa. He was wearing a plaid shirt and jeans, even though it was 85 degrees. His hair looked like that of an action figure and he spoke with a heavy Texas accent.

"All right! There he is, our fan of the year. Glad you made it."

He explained that I'd receive the award at midfield before kickoff. Sam and I would be on the Jumbotron while the PA announcer introduced me. After that, we'd return to our seats for the game itself. We had some time to kill, so he told us we could watch on the sidelines while the players warmed up. The Seahawks, that day's opponents, were across the field and we were right in front of the Chargers. I stood silently while future Hall of Famers like Drew Brees, Junior Seau, and LaDanian Tomlinson warmed up. Every now and then they'd stop and take a picture or sign an autograph, usually for a little kid.

I looked over at Sammy, who was decked out in my old Dan Fouts jersey. She asked if I wanted to try to meet any of the players.

"Nah. I think I'd rather talk to the coaches and ask why Brees isn't starting yet. It's the last game of the year and Doug Flutie is still in there."

Our escort clearly overheard only part of our conversation since he excitedly told us we could meet Flutie. He was just as short as he had looked on my television screen since the mid-1980s and couldn't get away from me fast enough after looking like he was having the time of his life standing between Sammy and me for a photo. Maybe he knew I wanted him benched that day.

"I think he's just kind of a dick," Sammy whispered.

I was falling more in love with her by the second. Before we knew it, the PA announcer was promising the crowd a "very special event before kickoff."

"Ladies and gentlemen, the Visa Hall of Fans honors each team's greatest fan with a special exhibit at the Pro Football Hall of Fame each year. This year's winner is ROB GROSS!" There was polite applause as I nervously clapped for myself. I glanced up at the scoreboard and saw my Stan Humphries jersey gleaming in the sun. Standing at midfield next to this giant Texan and my girlfriend was probably the closest I was going to get to the glory I imagined playing football at recess as a kid.

"Rob now lives in New York and writes an online newsletter!"

I understood why they wouldn't want to reveal that I'd never lived in San Diego. I also didn't get the vibe that my blog impressed the crowd. At least I would be able to explain my qualifications during my acceptance speech. I hadn't prepared anything, but knew I could explain my fanaticism pretty easily in words.

But before I knew it, the Visa rep was guiding Sammy and me off the field.

"What about my speech?"

"You don't give a speech. Maybe if you go Canton, they'll let you. But they've gotta game to play today."

I couldn't believe it. The crowd hadn't even understood why I'd won the award. We'd flown all the way out here and I wasn't going to be able to state my case. Just when I was about to explain my disappointment to Sam, I heard a voice behind me.

"Excuse me, Mr. Gross. I'm with Channel 10 here in San Diego. Would you mind answering a few questions for the camera?"

"Absolutely."

The brunette in the pantsuit shoved a microphone in front of me and asked for "my story."

"I don't view this award as so much about being the best fan this year, but rather a lifetime achievement award. This may not have been my strongest performance, but it's about my entire body of work. You know, like Clint Eastwood in *Unforgiven* or Al Pacino in *Scent of a Woman*."

I could see in the reporter's eyes that she had no idea what I was talking about.

"Well, how does it *feel* to receive this award, Rob?"

"I don't know. It's kind of like Anthony Michael Hall in *Sixteen Candles*. Now I'm king of the dipshits."

After she pulled the microphone away, she told me that while she couldn't use that last part, the rest was good. She promised to send me a video tape when the segment aired.

Sammy and I sat and watched the Chargers lose another game on the final play, but I was angrier about being denied the opportunity I thought I had earned. I looked down at the wooden plaque in my hand. It had the photo of me at the Super Bowl, face paint and all. The caption was a condensed version of the PA announcer's introduction. This didn't tell my full story. It didn't explain why I kept watching this heartbreaking team every week and it sure as hell didn't explain why I dragged Sammy out here. There was only one solution—I had to make the trip to Canton.

Join the Club?

"ROB, YOU *HAVE* to be kidding."

"What?"

"It looks like you're carrying a ventriloquist dummy with you."

What she was describing was my papier-mâché likeness of Dan Fouts. It had been the centerpiece at my bar mitzvah, even though it looked like an evil Claymation figure after all these years. Clearly, the caterers took their soccer player model, which looked more like a foosball figure and painted on Chargers colors. Instead of a helmet, they gave him a black mullet. In honor of my induction, I had scribbled a magic marker beard that made it look somehow even less like its intended subject.

"My parents did their best for 1984. I know it doesn't look that much like him."

"Yeah, that's not my issue with it. Let's just say I'm a very understanding girlfriend."

After finally getting our "lost ticket" to LA refunded, we were able to book a flight to Cleveland. The Hall of Fans induction would occur the same weekend that the new class of NFL players and coaches were inducted in Canton. The "Super Fans" would get to ride in their own float in the parade, get a group picture on the steps of the Hall, and give a speech in the basement ballroom. Only NFL officials and scattered media would be there, but there would be a podium with the NFL shield behind us. This felt like the lifetime achievement award I joked about in my television interview.

"I'm only going to put the Fouts figure on the float. It'll blend right in."

"Seamlessly," Sammy joked.

Neither of us knew quite how understanding she'd have to be since it was in the high 80s that August weekend. The parade float didn't give us much cover from the sun. At one point, I thought the Fouts figure was going to actually melt. Like being at midfield, it was surreal to be waving to onlookers thanks to my years of following this maddening football team. When we got back to our motel, many of the other "winners" were congregating in one of the conference rooms. I saw a few who I recognized from TV, like the Broncos fan who just wore a barrel and the "Big Dawg" from Cleveland. I'd never seen him without his rubber dog mask on and felt for a second like I was uncovering a secret identity. Of course, he was just a huge guy sweating his ass off underneath. I spotted the Seahawks and Eagles representatives starting to take off their face paint. Suddenly I felt like I was backstage at the circus. They probably just saw me as some guy in a Dan Fouts jersey with a disfigured piñata.

"Yo, Chargers guy! Come hang with us." It was the Big Dawg.

I turned to Sam and she shot me a look that said it was my call.

"You can even bring your doll," the Barrel Man joked.

"My girlfriend and I are gonna check out the Rock and Roll Hall of Fame in Cleveland."

There was no response. It was as if they couldn't imagine the weekend being about anything but being a football fan. I'd been to the Rock Hall, but knew Sam would also enjoy the exhibits. More importantly, I still couldn't figure out how I fit in with this weird collection of people.

We were walking between Janis Joplin's psychedelic Porsche and Jim Morrison's Cub Scout uniform when Sammy called me out for my ambivalence.

"Why are you afraid to hang out with the rest of the fans? It's like you're afraid you're going to become one of them."

"I guess you're right. Even the guys who brought their wives seem like they're at a comic book convention. I love the Chargers, but I'm not some costumed character."

"You once said something like that about the Dead. You can be obsessed with this stuff, and make no mistake, you definitely are, but that doesn't mean that's *who* you are. At least it doesn't have to. Plus, you hate when people assume all Deadheads are all carbon copy hippies."

She was right. The fact that Sam was still with me, literally and figuratively, proved that I wasn't defined by being a Chargers fan. I was running away from something that didn't even exist. I bet if I listened to other peoples' tales at the group dinner that night I'd find out that they each had their own backstory like I did.

"Before that dinner, let me show you the Dan Fouts bust back in Canton. Plus, I need to put together a good speech for tonight."

The 2001 Visa Fans of the Year had a series of tables reserved in the back room of one of Canton's biggest family-style pasta places. I looked around the table and saw that not one nominee had their "costume" on. We were seated in alphabetical order by NFL city, so I had a little time before they got to "S." I did get a weird flashback to my first day of kindergarten, but quickly extinguished it with a pint of Rolling Rock.

I heard some great stories. Some fans kept up the yearly fight because the team originally meant so much to their dads. Others loved the sense of community they felt each Sunday. There were a few who spoke about how their team got them through some tough times emotionally or medically. By the time it was my time to stand up, I started to wonder if I was even qualified to share my story.

"My name's Rob Gross. I haven't lived in San Diego a single day in my life. I don't have a game day character or anything . . ."

The Barrel Guy spoke up. "Just say what you feel. I was only kidding about the doll."

I was beginning to feel like Denzel Washington in the pre-battle prayer circle at the end of *Glory*. However, the Broncos representative, who was thankfully not wearing his barrel at dinner, had a point.

"Look, I've been a Chargers fan living in New York since I first saw Dan Fouts throw a bomb. But it's hard to root for a team when you have not one, but two, local ones you are shunning. I've been sneaking into bars to watch games since I got my first fake ID. Plus, there have been many years where my team has just sucked. I know many fanbases represented here tonight can relate. I'm looking at you, Cleveland Browns."

The room burst into laughter.

"Plus, I did this while attending 138 Grateful Dead concerts."

After the speech, the Big Dawg was the first to approach me. I worried was he'd be mad at my zinger, but he gave me a big hug.

I was immediately relieved, even if I felt like he could body slam me at any moment.

"Good job up there. You're definitely one of us. Rooting for a team that heartbreaking builds character. At least that's what I tell myself every year."

When I sat back down at the table, Sammy gave me a kiss.

"I hope you left some good bits for tomorrow."

Sunday's induction ceremony was in the basement of the Hall. It was essentially a ballroom with a rostrum and podium at the front. The official Pro Football Hall of Fame logo was on both the podium and a tapestry behind it. My performance at the bar got me bumped up on the speaking schedule for the induction ceremony. Many of the other Super Fans told me how much they enjoyed my speech and advocated for me to go early. With thirty other speakers, media coverage would drop off after the first half hour, they told me.

I was going up after the "Packalope," a Green Bay fan with antlers sprouting out of his helmet. Years later I'd see him on *The Daily Show* when the NFL banned his headgear due to an alleged security risk. Needless to say, he was a tough act to follow.

"First off, I'd like to thank Visa for not taking my credit card away. It's a matter of public record that I've attended countless games that I had no financial business going to. I'd also like to thank the Oakland Raiders because who among us hasn't had a victory against them as the lone highlight to their season."

After the subsequent laughter died down, I began what I saw as my closing argument.

"Speaking of the Raiders, everybody assumes they're outlaws. Outlaws live beyond laws, not necessarily against them. The 'Air Coryell' Chargers changed football with their passing attack. Their style brought amazing victories and equally heartbreaking losses. What's more outlaw than that? I don't know if I'm the biggest Chargers fan of this or any other year. I know how crazy it must seem to someone to care so much about something you cannot control. Everyone wants his or her team to win the Super Bowl. But there's something to be said for holding onto a dream no matter how insane it seems."

That got a nice round of applause.

"The first time I wrote to the Chargers, I never thought I'd get a response. But getting that personalized Dan Fouts autograph in the mail was the coolest feeling in the world. Sure, I now think the team sends me stuff just to avoid having to answer my coaching and personnel questions."

As the laughter built back up, I knew I needed a big finish.

"I'd like to thank not only the Pro Football Hall of Fame for admitting me but all the 'Super Fans.' I'm sure I've wished ill on every one of your teams at some point. But for today, at least, I feel like we're on the same side. Maybe not the Raiders, though."

As I stepped down from the podium to a mix of laughter and applause, an interviewer from Salon.com approached. He asked if he could get a little more background information on me and my story. As I waited for him to set up his tape recorder, Sam came up to hug me.

"You see? You just have to stop thinking so much!"

She was right. As I sat back down, though, I realized I now had a bigger problem.

I was going to have to ask her to marry me.

MAKES THE DREAM COME TRUE

THREE YEARS AFTER WE'D MET, I still couldn't find a single reason *not* to ask Sam to marry me. For the most part I'd been able to say "fuck the fear" each time I felt like I couldn't handle the anxiety that came with each step of the relationship. One of the things that made me love Sam so much was that she wasn't pressuring me to propose. But by now, even I felt like I was stalling a bit.

In addition to freelancing and keeping up my Chargers blog, I was toying with the idea of writing a book. I still had all my pieces from my writing class. It had been a workshop in "creative nonfiction," after all, so most of them had been loosely based on my life up until that point. I decided that Sam would be a good judge of whether I had anything worth publishing. I printed up a few of my old assignments and left them for her on the coffee table one Friday night when she was out with her friends.

I woke up the following morning to the rustling of paper. I regularly joked with Sam that she was a very aggressive reader while rifling through magazines, but this sounded like she was about to tear through the pages. We lived in a tri-level apartment with only the computer and television near our bed. I rubbed my eyes and saw Sammy sitting in my chair.

"What are you doing?"

"You really loved Kerry, huh?"

"Yeah, but that was almost ten years ago and why are you asking this now exactly?"

"*The Proper Potion*? You told me about the time you took mushrooms, but I didn't know it was such a big step in your relationship with her."

"Yeah, but who cares? Why does it matter?"

"Rob, you know I'm not one of those girls who gets jealous for no reason. But I really had no idea you guys were so serious."

"Sammy, it was college. Everything seemed so intense back then. Plus, it was a creative nonfiction class. It was clearly exaggerated for effect."

"I wouldn't know. I didn't really have any college boyfriends, remember?"

I got out of bed to console her, but she was already on her way downstairs.

"Rob, it's *fine*."

I knew that tone meant that it was the exact opposite of fine, but I suspected that it wasn't Kerry that Sam was upset about. Any time we discussed the idea of marriage, she made it pretty clear that she was ready. She knew that my heart was there, but my head hadn't quite caught up.

Her reaction to my piece on Kerry made perfect sense. She had a right to be hurt. I had put off proposing so long that she was bound to think that she was the reason. For advice, I decided to call the only other woman with whom I'd had a lasting relationship.

"Mom, I think I'm going to need help buying an engagement ring."

"Your father and I were wondering when you were going to smarten up. You're lucky Sam's as understanding as she is."

"I know, it's just scary. Marriage is so permanent."

"It won't be if you act like it's something you have to do. It'll never succeed that way. Believe me, your father and I work at it. But it's something we *want* to work at."

"I don't ever want to not be with Sam, but I get scared sometimes that I'm not ready."

"Rob, it's not marriage you're not ready for. You've always been hesitant to grow up. Remember how frightened you were the night before you first went to Camp Birchwood?"

"Yeah, but this is different . . ."

"Of course, but it's not Sam that scares you. Somehow you equate settling down to . . . settling."

Damn, she was good.

After giving me that final push, my mom agreed to lend me the money for the ring. I decided I would call Sammy's best friend Christine to find out what kind of diamond and proposal she would want.

"You know Sam. She's not going to want some big thing. Believe me, the fact that you're proposing will be more than enough."

That advice, and the fact that I didn't want Sam to have to continue to feel that I was holding out for any reason other than my own fear, was all that I needed. After going up to my parents' house to get the ring, I decided on the train ride home that I would just ask her as soon as we saw each other. I wasn't even sure she'd be back in the apartment when I got home. When I did, she was upstairs working on a paper for grad school. As soon as she looked into my eyes, she knew something was up. I walked over to her and got down on one knee.

"Oh . . . my . . . God . . ."

After she said yes, she immediately wanted to call her parents. I walked downstairs to grab a beer so she could have a little privacy. As I opened the fridge, I could hear her on the phone.

"Mom? You're not going to believe it . . . Yep! I know. I can't believe we're going to get married!"

Neither could I.

WORDS WHILE WASTED

SINCE THAT MAGICAL SUMMER at Camp Birchwood, alcohol had been my constant companion. So many great times were fueled by it. I may not have had a chemical dependency, but I couldn't imagine a night out without booze. With Sammy, drinking hadn't yet presented a problem. We first met at a bar, after all. Since we lived together, the worst she'd seen from me when we went out without her had been vomit on the toilet seat or melted cheese in the microwave.

Sammy and I were engaged for about three months when we went to see the Allmans with Money and DJ. The band played every year at the Beacon Theater uptown for almost the entire month of March. I always caught about three shows. It used to be only one show before Jerry's death, but I was clearly looking to fill that void. Sammy loved the Allmans and had even seen them the night Jerry died. The Beacon was an old Broadway theater with velvet seats and painted murals that looked more like an opera house than a concert hall. Once the ushers shut the doors and the lights went down, it was a full-on party.

It didn't seem like much was different between Sammy and I since my proposal. I knew we would soon be talking about guest lists, caterers, and wedding bands. That didn't scare me, but I knew greater change was coming. Somehow, I had become the most "adult" among my friends. I knew Sam and I would eventually be discussing having kids and probably moving out of the city to raise them. That night I didn't want to think about anything serious. The Allmans came out to the Tom Waits song from the opening credits of *The Wire* and just started wailing into a classic from their first album.

The four of us had some beers and shots in us already and the music complemented the buzz perfectly. I flipped my Chargers hat backward and grabbed Sammy's left hand. As I was shuckling back and forth like a rabbi, I could feel the diamond from her engagement ring digging into my clasped palm.

As the set wore on, Money and DJ kept going back to the bar to bring us back drinks. After the third round Sammy yelled into my ear.

"Can you ask them to bring me water from now on? It's still a Thursday and I can't be showing up hungover tomorrow."

"Sure, but the show's been awesome. I might just call in sick to school tomorrow. It's a Friday, anyway."

When they slowed down the set with some blues numbers, Sammy sat down next to Money and DJ. I couldn't understand why. The band was cooking. No one our age really sat in their seats at an Allmans show. Since we were in the center of our row,

I heard someone scream behind me when the band launched into a long instrumental to close the set.

"Down in front!"

I turned around and saw a massively overweight guy in a tie-dye smoking a bowl. It was a pretty reasonable request, especially since we were in the balcony, as opposed to the floor. But before I knew it, the words flew out of my mouth:

"It's the Allmans! What's the point of sitting? Didn't you come here to have fun?"

"I am, but I'd like to see the stage at least for a song. You haven't sat down once. It's not like you have to prove anything."

Sam grabbed my hand. "Let it go. Set break is coming up, anyway."

I begrudgingly sat down, but not before I told the guy what a dick he was. I knew there was no chance that he'd try to fight me. His girth and my five shots of bourbon clearly provided me with the added courage. As soon as the lights came on, Money and Sam tried to beat the lines for the bathroom while DJ and I went to the bar.

"Luca," he said, "you gotta maintain the level with drinking."

I'd never heard such talk of moderation from DJ.

"What are you fuckin' talking about?"

"Pacing's never been your thing, but it's all about peaks and valleys. You're starting to become like the alpine climber from the game on *The Price Is Right*. You just go off the edge."

"That's the stupidest analogy I've ever heard," I said. "How many nights have we partied together? When I've had too much, I just go home."

"What, the 'Irish Exit' where you don't even say goodbye? I saw the look on Sam's face during the first set. I don't even have a girlfriend, but I can sense trouble coming."

Almost on cue, Sam returned.

"Rob, I'm really tired. I have to work tomorrow. I'm gonna head home."

"The second set's about to start. You can't leave now."

"You have your friends here. Why does it matter? I'm not leaving you, just the show."

"Come on, Sam! It's the Allmans. How can you leave?"

"Very easily in this case. I'm fucking exhausted."

"You can't bail on me!"

"Rob, you're drunk. Honestly, seeing you get even more so for the second set isn't exactly making me want to suck it up and stay."

"I can't believe you're taking off. What ever happened to the girl I met at McSwiggan's? She'd never bail. You're the girl I promised to share my life with after all these years of being afraid. I really put all my eggs in one basket with you."

"What did you just say?"

The second it came out of my mouth, I knew it was wrong. My attempt to suppress both my mistake and my drunkenness made me even more aggressive.

"Is this what it's gonna be like when we get married? You're just going to be that girl that leaves the show early? You say it's okay for me to stay, but you know you're just going to make me feel bad tomorrow."

None of the things I was saying were nice or true which was why Sam started to head towards the stairwell. My inebriation finally took over as I stumbled trying to catch up to her. I reached out and grabbed her shoulder. As my hand clamped down on her shoulder socket, she turned around with her face contorted in fury.

"GET . . . OFF . . . OF . . . ME!"

The look on Sam's face was a combination of anger, hurt, and disappointment. I had no idea how I'd gotten to this point, but it was too late to stop it. As if on cue, I suddenly felt a hand on *my* shoulder.

"That's it, buddy. You gotta go."

I didn't even have a chance to get a good look at the security guard before he slapped his other hand on me and started guiding me down the stairs.

"Get the fuck off me! You can't kick me out. Sammy, tell him who I am!"

Sam ambled up beside us and mumbled that I was her fiancé. But the hurt and anger on her face suggested she was far from proud of it at that moment. The security guard clearly saw it too because he kept shoving me out the door. Before I knew it, we were out on the street as the cabs whizzed down Broadway.

"I can't believe they kicked me out. I gotta text DJ and Money."

"They saw what happened, believe me. I'm sure they weren't surprised."

We quickly hailed a taxi and climbed into the backseat.

"Rob, instead of being upset about being kicked out, maybe you should be worried about what caused it."

"Yeah, I know I'm really drunk. So what?"

"You said you put all your eggs in one basket. You acted like me wanting to go home was some reflection on *our* decision to get married. Do you have any idea what you looked like coming after me in there?"

"I may be fucked up," I protested, "but I wasn't the one who wanted to leave."

"Maybe you should ask yourself why you're so angry right now. It's about more than being wasted."

With that, Sam announced to the driver that we would be making two stops.

"I'm going to stay at Christine's downtown and call in sick into my internship tomorrow."

"I thought going in was so important!"

"I need the space. You do too, even if you can't see it right now. No matter how fucked up you are, this stuff is coming from somewhere. You need to figure out why you said that stuff, *no matter what happens with us.*"

Those last words were the ones I kept replaying in my head after getting out of the cab and dejectedly heading upstairs. I didn't even approach the bed. It was too depressing to lie down by myself. I laid on the couch to think, but quickly passed out. When I woke up at 4:00 AM, I forgot for a moment what had happened. Once I realized I was alone, it all came back to me. I still couldn't believe that Sam hadn't come back to our apartment. I considered trying her cell, but figured she wouldn't pick up. I had never seen her so pissed.

My head was throbbing. DJ was right that I needed to scale back on the drinking. I used to think that it opened me up to the magical possibilities of any given evening, but maybe it was starting to become the destination itself. I got so easily sucked into the "high" of the perfect experience that I overlooked that most of life is just a normal Thursday. If you were lucky enough to be with your fiancée at a concert, you shouldn't fuck it up by getting completely wasted and projecting onto to her. This *was* about more than booze. Sam wanting to leave was evidence that I was numbing myself to the frightening reality that things were really good between us, but that the only way it would stay that way was for me to keep my fears in check.

I thought I had my anxiety about getting married under control. Of course, I thought the same thing about my drinking. Clearly, I was wrong on both counts. I was already worrying about leaving the city, having kids, and leaving behind the guy I had been in college. At that moment, I wondered if I wasn't some sort of sad caricature of that once again.

Whatever I was worried about, I needed to deal with it. If it was something that would benefit from a discussion with Sam, that needed to happen. Leaning on her was much different than pushing her away. I looked at my watch and saw that it was 6:00 AM. There was no way I could go into work. I used to be afraid of any relationship I couldn't get out of. Now I was more terrified that Sam would leave me. After calling in sick to school, I tried her cell. It went right to voicemail. I waited for what seemed like forever and tried again, but it had only been fifteen minutes.

My first instinct was to keep calling, but that was just the sort of obsessive thinking that had gotten me to this point. I was able to wait about thirty minutes this time. Then I waited another half an hour and another after that. Finally, at about 9:00 AM, Sam called back. I could feel my heart beating in my throat as I picked up the phone.

"Rob?"

"Yes?"

"I'm still not even sure I'm ready to talk to you."

"So why did you call?"

"You've dialed my number about twenty times in the last three hours."

"Oh yeah."

"Before you say anything, you need to listen. You made me feel like absolute shit last night. You acted like somehow I pushed you into proposing and we both know that isn't even *remotely* the case. I've never been this hurt before and the fact that you were the one who caused it is what's most painful. I don't know if those words came from some place deep down but I won't ever put up with this again. You won't have to worry about us getting married anymore because I'll be gone."

"I know."

"When I get home later, I need to lie down. Even though I don't want to have some big talk about this today you need to know how angry I still am. We didn't get this far making it all about you and your fears. Things won't always be only on your terms. If that's what you want, you're going to find yourself all alone."

"I'm so sorry, Sammy. I really do love you so much."

"I do, too. But things need to change."

"I understand."

"And Rob?"

"What?"

"I think you might want to lay off the shots for a while."
"No fucking kidding."

A Promise Worth Making, Finally

IT TOOK SOME REAL EFFORT to monitor my drinking, but that was easy compared to getting Sam to trust me again. I knew I had betrayed her at the Beacon. She had never made me feel badly for my anxieties about committing to her, yet I still threw it back in her face all in one night. I didn't know how to make things right. Any more conversations about our relationship would probably backfire. I needed something to show her how much I appreciated her and that I was really ready to take the next step.

Once I figured out what I planned to do, I ran it by Money and DJ. After seeing me unravel at the Allmans, they were the only ones who understood how important this was.

"I'm buying us all Springsteen tickets for the Rochester show."

Sammy and I had seen Bruce a few times together. The look of pure joy on her face for three-plus hours was even more infectious than hearing her talk about "The Boss" on the night we met. The Rochester show was the final stop of Bruce's tour and I thought including her on a pilgrimage to the site of so many adventures that preceded her would be the perfect gesture. I knew Sam would be psyched to go, but I was also asking her best friend Christine to come along beforehand to make it even more enticing for her to say yes.

We all met at JFK airport after our respective work days. Our flight, less than an hour long, was scheduled to get us to Rochester with plenty of time to spare. Since we were only staying for the night, we all agreed to only bring carry-on bags. We didn't want anything left to chance. After getting through the security gate, however, we were immediately struck by the "DELAYED" designation next to our flight on the board. The air came out of all five of us simultaneously. DJ pulled himself together first and asked the woman behind Jet Blue counter what the cause was.

"Sir, it's snowing in Rochester."

"It's *always* snowing in Rochester," he quickly replied.

She explained that the blizzard was only now tapering off and that an announcement would be made when a departure time was determined. As we made our way over to the bar, I could feel the apprehension among our group. It was Sammy I was most concerned about. The weather conditions were obviously beyond my control, but she and I *really* needed this trip.

I pulled her close to me at the bar and gave her a soft kiss on the forehead. When she looked up at me, I could see her cheeks were a little scrunched up in that way that meant she was fighting to keep some disappointment at bay. I had no idea if we were going to get to the show on time, but I knew I wanted this to happen more than anything.

This would normally be where I would have a drink as I tried to figure out how to tell her my thoughts. After the Beacon, however, I wisely decided to take an alcoholic hiatus. Fortunately, Money slapped me on the shoulder to announce that the flight was now scheduled to leave in an hour.

We immediately started lining up at the gate, only to be told by the woman behind the counter that we needed to sit back down.

I stopped myself before screaming, and calmly responded, "What is it now?"

"Sir, we are waiting on six wheelchairs to make it to the gate."

I couldn't be mad at someone with a disability, but six wheelchairs? Our trips to visit Sam's parents in South Florida didn't have that many. I simply sat down with my crew of increasingly discouraged voyagers and waited . . .

and waited . . .

AND WAITED.

The people who were responsible for finding the last six wheelchairs in JFK airport were moving slower than the people who actually needed those wheelchairs. Finally, after fifteen minutes, they ushered us onto the plane.

We were halfway to Rochester and Bruce was scheduled to hit the stage in two hours. With Sammy next to me and against the window, I looked down the row. DJ, Money, and Christine were all smiles. The captain said the snow had lightened up and that we would land on time. It seemed like the worst was behind us.

I turned to Sam, who put her head on my shoulder.

"I really appreciate you putting this together, Rob."

"Let's just make sure you're on the floor by the opening song." As the plane was taxiing, we were all so pumped that I was afraid we'd run the flight attendants over just to get off the plane. By the time six wheelchairs finally arrived at the gate, we had less than an hour. We decided to split up. Money and DJ would run over to the rental car desk, while Sammy, Christine, and I would grab cash at the ATM. When we found the one bank machine in the entire airport, we were instantly grateful that there was only one woman waiting to use it. However, my gratitude quickly turned to frustration as I watched her punch what looked like twenty different buttons.

What the fuck could she be doing? If I entered my birthday, social security number, bank account number, and jersey numbers of my four favorite Chargers, it *still* wouldn't have equaled the amount of data this woman seemed to be entering. The final straw occurred only after she took out her card and then proceeded to put an entirely different one in the slot.

I was about to sarcastically ask this woman if she had some off-shore money she was moving around when Sammy stepped in.

"We're sorry. It's just that we flew here from New York City to see Bruce Springsteen and we're running a little late."

I assumed she wouldn't understand or care about our dilemma

but loved that Sam was willing to try. Needless to say, I was surprised by the response.

"*The Boss* is in Rochester? By all means you can go first."

When we got to the rental car counter, Money and DJ were in active negotiations with the agent.

"Listen," Money said, "all we need is a car to get us from here to the War Memorial as quickly as possible. I don't see what the holdup is for."

"If you are going to decline the insurance on the vehicle, we must have the name of your personal carrier."

"Fine. Martin Van Nostrand," Money replied.

"And what agency is Mr. Van Nostrand with?"

"The Travelers."

The agent scribbled this information down as Money grabbed the keys off the counter. As we ran out to the parking lot, I screamed to him: "Dude, when did you get your own insurance agent?"

"I didn't. That was Kramer's dermatologist alias from *Seinfeld*."

Luckily, DJ worked for a prominent hotel chain and got us a good deal on the hotel directly across from the arena. We got there right at 8:00 PM and threw our bags behind the counter. I don't think we even officially checked in.

We ran across the street and up the stone steps, hoping to get in just as Bruce hit the stage. We got through the turnstiles to see that the hallways of the old hockey arena, where I'd last seen Sinatra a decade earlier, were packed. I didn't hear any music coming from inside, so I knew we were okay. Since all the floor seats were general admission, Sammy and I wandered through the tunnel to check it out.

The Rochester War Memorial, by then renamed the Blue Cross Arena, held about 11,000 people. When we emerged under the bright lights hanging from the steel rafters, it just looked like a big gym. The roadies were still climbing above the stage, which was flanked by billboards for WCMF FM and Genesee Beer. We had made it.

After finding a spot that was equidistant from the stage and the bathrooms at the rear of the floor, we saw no sign of Sammy and Christine. When the lights went down and the crowd erupted, I was about to go looking for them when I felt a hand on my shoulder. I turned around to see Sammy with Christine next to her.

"You didn't think I'd miss it, did you?"

Before I could answer, Bruce and the band hit the stage to thunderous applause. The show was a full-throttle monster even by Springsteen standards. As the lights bathed the crowd, we all sang along with The Boss he began "No Surrender."

I grabbed Sam's hand and felt the diamond from her engagement ring on my palm. I smiled to her to assure her that I could handle what it represented. As Clarence Clemons launched into his first sax solo of the night, I turned towards her. As I was about open my mouth, Sam shouted into my ear "I love you, too."

As great a night as we all had in Rochester, one worry kept creeping into my head.

How was I going to find a wedding band who could do a good "Rosalita?"

JUMP A LITTLE HIGHER AS WE REACH THE MORNING LIGHT

"ROB, SAMANTHA, TELL ME HOW the two of you met."

We were sitting in the apartment of the rabbi we hoped would marry us. He spoke in that specific cadence that only rabbis have where everything sounds like a question. It just so happened in this case that he was actually asking one.

I let Sam field this one.

"We were taking a class in history together."

This piqued his interest. "History is very important. What kinds of things do you enjoy doing together?"

I instantly thought of that day in my apartment when we both realized we were both in love. "We both like music and seeing it performed live. But I think we're both happiest just hanging around with each other."

"That's so true, Rob," he said. "You need to be comfortable with your partner. Samantha, how would you describe Rob? Why do you want to spend your life with him?"

"Like he said, we have so much fun together. Rob makes me laugh, but not just in the way that he makes *everyone* laugh. He always knows just the right thing to say when I need it the most. I always feel loved by him."

I grabbed Sam's hand. While I knew there was no way I could top that, I also knew I didn't have to. As I began speaking, I realized my words were more for Sam than for the rabbi.

"All my life, I thought that finding the perfect girl would make everything else in my life instantly perfect. Of course, I never considered that the life I'd be sharing would be the one of an adult. I don't always like dealing with the everyday stuff that comes with being a grown-up, but there's no one I could imagine myself doing it with but her."

I didn't need to even look at Sam after finishing. I could just tell by the way she squeezed my hand that I had nailed it.

"You both seem to really know and appreciate each other. Is there anything else about yourselves that you'd like to share?"

I jumped right in. "Well, now that you mention it. There is this football team . . ."

The way Sam squeezed my hand this time told me to stop.

It took a little while after that to find a band that would play our requests (beyond just the Springsteen) as well as the standard Jewish wedding fare. Sam agreed on one Dead song, as long as it was under five minutes. Stealing a move from the protagonist in

High Fidelity, I decided to make a CD of the rest of our favorite songs. We knew we had found the right band when they began the negotiations asking which three songs we did *not* want them to play. We knew we had to include some prerequisite disco tunes, but agreed on "YMCA," "Hot, Hot, Hot," and "Last Dance." In fact, the band seemed cool enough that I was able to call them later on with a special request:

I wanted to join them onstage for "Rosalita" and surprise Sam.

"Rosalita" not only sounds like a party set to music, but the lyrics are written from the point of view of a guy singing to a girl's parents about their future together. I thought it was perfect.

It was at McSwiggan's, after I asked Money and DJ to be my best men, that I revealed my plan to them.

"You've gotta do it," Money agreed.

"Luca," DJ reminded me, "you know it's not going to be like singing on the subway."

He was right, but I knew Sam wouldn't expect it. Despite my lack of vocal ability, I knew it would mean a lot to her.

Sam's parents agreed with us that we should hold the wedding at a Long Island hotel so everyone could celebrate and sleep in the same place. After the rehearsal dinner, we both had one last night before making it official. She and her bridesmaids ended up taking a few bottles of wine back to her suite.

"Enjoy yourself," Sam said. "Just don't overdo it, please. Tell Money and DJ that I expect you to show up in one piece tomorrow, and I'm not talking about that party you guys had in college."

All my friends were fine just hanging in my suite. When Money asked how I wanted to spend the night, I thought it over for a few seconds.

"Honestly, I'd like to hang out and watch *Old School* and the Tahoe scenes of *Godfather II*. If we could also get a good bottle of tequila, it'd be perfect."

Money convinced the hotel bartender to sell him a bottle of

top shelf 100% agave tequila, also a rarity in those days. I'm sure they didn't let him off easy on the price, but it just made the effort that much more appreciated.

DJ was in charge of finding a DVD player. The hotel didn't have one, so he actually went to the nearest Best Buy and came back with one within the hour. By that time, we were pretty deep into the tequila and ready to enjoy the movie.

I had already seen *Old School* three times in the theater that year and owned the DVD. I thought it would be the perfect movie to watch. It was great to watch twenty of my closest friends from all stages of my thirty-two years enjoy it together. Some were sitting on the floor, others at the foot of my bed and some standing. As my tequila buzz set in, it occurred to me that the movie was about three guys who attempt to revive fraternity life after college. It hadn't been quite as funny doing that for real. At least it had gotten me here, or maybe that happened in spite of my desire to keep my college world going.

About half the room decided to call it a night after the movie was over. The rest remained for *Godfather II*. I poured myself a glass of tequila and leaned back in the executive desk chair. Before too long, I found myself shouting out the dialogue for entire scenes. Occasionally someone would throw in a line or two, but I was mostly putting on a show by myself. Watching a movie where you know every word is like comfort food. You know exactly what to expect and are never disappointed. By the time the middle-aged Michael Corleone gazed onto his empty Lake Tahoe compound and the credits rolled, it was close to 3:00 AM. The only thing left to do was get a little sleep before getting married.

The 23rd was a beautiful August day. Sammy was getting her hair and makeup done along with all her bridesmaids. Once we spoke and she was sure I was ready to go, she told me I was free for the afternoon. I caught up with my friends for a few poolside drinks. DJ tried to clear out any random guests by throwing a candy bar into the pool, á la *Caddyshack*. It didn't work, but the other guests got the reference and loved his effort.

After I got into my tux, Sam and I met with both our respective families. She had her veil on when I first saw her in the dress. I knew she looked beautiful but had to lift it up to tell her.

"I love you, beekeeper," I whispered.

"Now I know you're ready," she said. We signed our *ketubah* with the rabbi and were legally married after doing so, but that wasn't what everyone came out to Long Island to witness.

Once Sammy and I were together under the *chuppah*, the rabbi began addressing our guests.

"I am wrapping Rob and Samantha in the *tallit*, the prayer shawl, of Rob's grandfather. Today, August 23rd, would actually have been his birthday."

My mom was the one who reminded me of this once we had set the date. I couldn't help but think about him taking me to *Animal House* and everything that had gotten me here. Sam looked over at me and could tell I was in deep thought. I didn't want her to worry that I was freaking out so I pulled her close and whispered in her ear.

"I have never been surer of anything in my entire life."

The smile she gave me had me walking on air for the remainder of the night.

The ceremony ended with the breaking of the glass.

"This will probably the last time you get to put down your foot in your marriage," the rabbi joked.

I'm sure he used that line in every wedding he did, but it still worked.

After a "MAZEL TOV!" from all, we were coming down the aisle to celebrate for the cocktail hour. Afterwards, we would begin the reception after being officially introduced as husband and wife. We agreed on the theme from *Airplane!*, Sam's favorite movie and a genius selection. I had made an audio cassette of the first five minutes of the film for the band to use and had it cued up perfectly. When the bandleader, though, told everyone to give a huge applause for "Mr. and Mrs. Rob Gross," that wasn't what came blasting over the PA.

"Da-dum, Da-dum, Da-dum, Da-dum, Da-dum, Da-dum."

It was the theme from *Jaws*.

The bandleader must have rewound the tape to the beginning of my *Airplane!* tape, where that parody occurs.

"The theme from *Jaws*, ladies and gentlemen. That would have been perfect for my first marriage."

Sammy and I were both laughing as we strolled onto the dance floor. As we began dancing to "Love Minus Zero/No Limit," we looked into each other's eyes. We didn't need words to express our feelings, especially since Bob Dylan had beat us to it. The band did a great job, even entertaining our older guests. They parodied Earth, Wind, And Fire to sing "Ba de ya, the salad's on the table." We didn't know that one was coming.

At the end of the night, when I came up to thank the band, they had another surprise for me.

"I don't know if we're gonna get to the Springsteen song," the bandleader said.

"What? We agreed on it and I even bought you guys the sheet music."

"Yeah, it's a pretty long song and all. We gotta take a break. It's a union thing."

I walked over to the bar in a daze. Even if Sammy never knew about my grand gesture, I couldn't stand the idea that she'd be denied a Bruce song at the very least. I went over the bar and joined Money and DJ.

"Great party, Luca. My compliments to Sam's parents," said DJ.

"I don't think they're gonna play Bruce," I glumly replied.

Money was apoplectic. "No. We'll get 'em to do it."

"Thanks, but it's not a big deal."

"Fuck that," Money said. "It's a genius idea and Sam will love it. They're playing 'Rosalita,' don't worry."

As he and DJ left to find the bandleader, I sipped my drink and felt thankful these guys still had my back. Of course, part of me was also worried what they would try to do to get the band to comply.

Sure enough, the bandleader came back from his break with an announcement.

"We have a special song that Rob has asked to play for Samantha. He's actually going to join us on it."

I passed Money and DJ on my way up to the stage. I was about to give them a hug when the guitar, drums, and saxophone kicked in. I could see Sam was in shock. She obviously recognized the song but didn't expect me to get behind the microphone and scream, "Spread out now Rosie . . ."

With each verse I got a little more confident and everyone was jumping up and down on the dance floor. When I sang the verse about only being there for fun, I reached out my hand. Sam's friends had to give her a last-second push, but she ran up join me. Before too long, we were sharing the mic. She even took a verse on her own before it was over. By that point, I also spotted a few girls on their dates' shoulders.

"I can't believe you did this," Sam said. "I love you."

"Me too, I just hope we don't get sued by the wedding band union."

"I gotta hand it to you guys," the bandleader said. "I have *never* seen a wedding end like this. Your marriage better be one hell of an encore."

I had fought both for and against this day for my entire life. But as we held hands and stepped off the stage, I realized that it wasn't the end of the trip. More than an encore, this was going to be an entirely new journey. Thank God I had finally found someone to take it with.

GROWIN' UP?

IT TOOK A WHILE AFTER GETTING MARRIED to notice the difference. We got a joint bank account and changed our W-4 forms, but it still felt like regular "Rob and Sam." We went to work, spent some nights at home in our apartment and others out with our friends. Somewhere along the way, however, it felt like we didn't fit in the city any more.

"It just feels off," I admitted to her.

"I know," she said. "It's like we're watching everyone else live when we should be moving on to something else."

I didn't plan to live in New York City for the rest of my life, but I hadn't thought about moving back to the suburbs, either. At least Long Island would be new for me. Sam's parents were in the process of moving to Florida full time and had already sold her childhood home. However, they owned a condo in a "55 and over" community that they were planning to hold onto for a year. As weird as living with them there would be, they were rarely home and we could live on our own without paying rent. Our lease expired in June, so I'd have an entire year to look for a teaching job on Long Island. Sam could get her Master's in Social Work and find an office job. Of course, that would change if she got pregnant.

It's not as if we were talking about having kids yet, but I knew it was coming. That shared subconcious admission was probably the reason for both of us wanting to move out of Manhattan. Neither of us had been raised in a city and we couldn't imagine doing it as parents. It would have been well beyond our means, anyway. Even though we both had friends who were also married by this point, they all still lived in the city. We would be the first to leave.

Our last year in the city felt strange. My friends were

supportive but clearly apprehensive. Money vocalized it to me one night over beers.

"Do want to eat at the Olive Garden every week? Before you know it, you'll be spending your money on a lawn mower. It won't even be the kind you push, either. You'll have to get one of those riding mowers you sit on. Is that what you want?"

"Of course not. I know it's crazy how much has changed since the night I met Sam. I don't like change, but it's not like I was going to live in the city forever. I'm going to come back to see you guys. I don't expect I'm going to become friends with my neighbors, especially since they'll be retirees."

Money laughed, but seemed to understand. "I know, Luca. It would just be great to have you guys around for a while. A riding mower would actually be kind of cool."

"I don't think I'll be buying any appliances yet. It's not for a year, anyway."

That ended up making it more difficult, rather than less. We had fun, but I always felt the clock ticking. After all, I'd been in Manhattan for ten years. I realized it wasn't going to be as easy as I thought to say goodbye when I began looking for a teaching job on Long Island. I was fortunately able to get some interviews set up by springtime. Things were moving along well, which was when I started to feel that familiar anxiety. Of course, it manifested itself in a different form.

Sam came home from grad school one night to find me sitting alone in the apartment listening to The Doors. I was drinking tequila and staring at the channel guide on the TV.

"Uh, what's up Rob?"

"Nothing."

"Something's up, clearly. I've had a long day, but I'll be more than happy to listen if you feel like talking."

"I don't know, Sammy. Things seem to going well looking for a job, but it's just scary that we're really going to be on our own."

"I know," she said. "But unfortunately, life doesn't always

wait for you to feel one hundred percent ready. You've actually been moping around for a while now, although this is more than a little dramatic."

"Hey! At least I've been watching the booze. This is my first."

"I appreciate that, but monitoring your drinking isn't something you decided to do just for me. In fact, neither is moving. You think it's so easy for me, by the way? I've lived in Manhattan as long as you have."

"I never really thought of that," I confessed.

"That's because it's not always about you and your fears. Are you worried about the type of commitment this represents? *Still*? I've got news for you, Rob. You bought your ticket for this ride a long time ago."

After that conversation, I started to deal a little better. At the very least, I made a concerted effort to put Sam's feelings ahead of mine every now and then. We had some great nights out with our friends before moving day. None was better than the night before the 2004 NFL draft. After another last place finish, the Chargers had the first overall pick. It was clear they planned to pick Eli Manning, brother of Peyton. Eli wasn't necessarily the best quarterback in the 2004 draft, with Ben Roethlisberger and Philip Rivers also available. But Manning was the safest pick and the Bolts couldn't afford to fuck this up. However, Manning patriarch Archie, once a quarterback on a perennially lousy New Orleans Saints team, announced that there was no chance his son would ever play for the Chargers.

No one knew how maddeningly bad the San Diego Chargers were at that point more than me, but who the fuck was he to point it out? Like Boon said of the pledges in *Animal House*, only we can do that. In this case, "we" meant the fans—and what was the point of winning Fan of the Year if not to use your power to right such a wrong?

The draft was held at Madison Square Garden every year back then and all the top picks stayed at a swanky hotel downtown. I knew this because DJ set up their teleconferencing equipment. He decided not to tell me until the night before at McSwiggan's.

"Luca, I know how you get. Shit, you almost killed us before ever getting to the stadium in Cleveland. I need this job and they can't find out I'm letting you harass the draftees."

"DJ, I'm surprised at you. I'm not going to harass the draftees, just one."

"Somehow that doesn't make me feel any better."

I ordered us a round and decided to give a try. I didn't think for a second, however, that the switchboard operator would put me through.

"Hullo?"

"Is this Eli?"

"Uh, yeah."

I had no idea what I wanted to say. I knew I couldn't curse him out no matter tempting. "I represent the San Diego Chargers Fan Coalition and it's not cool to trash the team through the media this way."

I really wasn't prepared for him to listen to me. I couldn't believe he hadn't hung up already.

"Okay . . ."

"And . . . that's all I wanted you to know."

"Have a good night now."

That *bastard*.

"Karma's a bitch," I said as I hung up the phone.

The Chargers drafted him the following day only to trade him to the Giants, for whom he won two Super Bowls. Ben Roethlisberger also won a couple for the Steelers. The Bolts ended up with Philip Rivers, who may very well make the Hall of Fame without having reached a Super Bowl. So I guess karma actually isn't a bitch, unless you're a Chargers fan.

LIVING IN DOUBT

BY THE FALL, WE HAD SETTLED IN to life on Long Island. The condo had more than enough space for us, especially with Sam's parents gone most of the time. I still had to put a lot of posters, books, bobbleheads, and other ephemera in storage. Once we bought a house of our own, I would rescue them from captivity.

At least that's what I told myself, as things between Sam and I were going well. I tried to keep my promise of being honest about my feelings as we settled into life outside the city. I found a job teaching high school social studies and Sam worked in a real estate office. It was on the nights she had grad school and I was home alone that I most noticed the difference in living in the suburbs.

"Except you didn't do anything while I was at class when we lived in the city," she'd say.

"But I knew that I could. I could go out with my friends or go see a movie."

"You weren't going out much during the week this past year and you can still go to the movies."

"Well I can't sneak in beers like I used to. You have to drive everywhere out here. And we can't get pizza at 4:00 AM either."

"I'll admit I do miss the pizza," she joked. "It hasn't been easy for me, either. I miss my friends. Those weekends we've gone back into the city always remind me how much. But did you really think we were going to start a family in Manhattan? "

"Yeah, you're right."

"Speaking of which . . ."

I knew Sam's family had a history of miscarriages. The few times we'd discussed when we would start "trying," she reminded me that her mom really didn't think she'd be able to bring Sam to term.

"That's why she still calls me her 'little miracle,'" she joked. "I'm sure it will take a while for me to even *get* pregnant."

Other than having sex, I didn't even know what "trying" meant. As sad as it sounds, Sam explained the ovulation process to me. The ensuing intercourse during that first attempt was pretty awkward. When we were done, we both joked about it.

"I hope we don't have go through that too many more times," I said with a smile on my face.

I never expected Sam to emerge from the bathroom one snowy Saturday with a home pregnancy test in her hand and say, "You're not going to believe this . . ."

I wanted to blurt out that I thought we were going to have a lot more time to deal with this. I wanted to say I was misled. Sam had said it would take a while to get pregnant. I wanted to say a lot of the things that were bouncing around my head. However, I wisely decided to say none of them. The idea of trying to sift through my fears was exhausting, so I decided to take a nap.

I experienced the kind of sleep you have when you're just trying to avoid reality, but at least it kept me from purging all my selfish anxiety-fueled feelings. When I woke up, we calmly discussed the next steps.

"I know this isn't the timetable we discussed, Rob. I'll make a doctor's appointment this week just to confirm. Underneath all your fears, I hope you're still happy too."

"Of course I am, sweetie. It's just . . ."

"I know," she said.

The visit to her OB-GYN confirmed that she was due in October. We agreed that we'd find out the gender beforehand.

"I like to know how things are going to turn out."

"No shit," she joked. "This is one of the few times you'll be able to do that."

The weekend after we were told that we would be having a girl, we went into the city to celebrate with all our friends. Since Sam obviously wasn't drinking, I unfortunately had enough for both of us. I was starting to imbibe more each time I came into the city since leaving it after doing a good job initially of moderating. I wanted to make the most of those nights out, but ended up just getting way more fucked up that necessary. It didn't help that now I had to crash on one of my friends' couches before driving home the following morning. Since Sam wasn't around on those nights, I didn't feel the additional need to monitor my drinking. It was clearly building up, however, as was my anxiety about being a dad.

When Sam told me she wanted to go home early that Saturday night, I didn't unravel like I had at the Beacon. It was in the cab on the way to the hotel we had booked downtown that Sam could tell I wasn't dealing well with my conflicting feelings.

"What gives, Rob? Please don't tell me you get this fucked up when you come in without me.""Not exactly." My slurring wasn't doing me any favors. "It's just happening all so fast. I mean, I'm going to have a daughter."

"*You're* going to have a daughter? Look at this stomach. I think I deserve at least partial credit. Seriously, you're not in a Judd Apatow movie. You never were."

It was at that moment that the taxi we were in stopped short. The car in front of us had slammed its brakes at the red light.

"What the fuck! She's pregnant!"

The cab driver apologized profusely and I turned to Sam. She looked pissed, but I couldn't understand why. My outburst had somehow intensified the effects of all the booze I had consumed, as I was starting to feel really fucked up. We rode the rest of the way to the hotel in silence. When we got inside, Sam began talking.

"Honestly, were you really worried about my well-being back there? If you were you'd pay a little more attention to my feelings. I know you're pretty wasted, which is more than a little concerning. It's not about the drinking; it's that it's pretty obvious you're doing it as a way of not dealing."

"I know," I said. I sounded like a chastened child. Some of that was the booze, but I knew she was right.

"Look where you are. Look where *we* are. What are you really so afraid of?"

I didn't think before answering, which was usually a bad decision for me.

"I guess I'm most afraid of not having anything to be afraid of. I've always feared getting in over my head with a girl and then having to get myself out."

"Do you want out of this?"

"Absolutely not and that's what's frightening."

"Welcome to adulthood," Sam joked. "Now get some sleep. You need to drive us home in the morning. My entire body aches. I'm pregnant, in case you didn't hear the lunatic in the cab."

THE PRIZE I SEE IN THOSE EYES

SARAH WAS DUE TO ARRIVE in late October. We named her after Sam's grandmother and I was also happy that she wouldn't have some trendy name. Once we went past the due date, however, I started to panic.

"Rob, it's been one day. It happens all the time. I'm the person you should be worried about. I hate looking and feeling this way."

"You're right, sweetie. You look great, by the way."

"I'm thirty pounds overweight and you're not that good of a liar. I don't know how some women like being pregnant, unless it's just to lie in bed. Let's just go out for dinner. We can even have Mexican. Also, a margarita might mellow you out a bit. I mean *one*, though, since I need you to drive home." When we got home, Sam just wanted to lie down and enjoy what was left of our Friday. Her stomach started hurting her, but she assured me it was just due to the spicy food. When the pain didn't get better, she suggested I give the doctor a call. I was on the phone with Long Island Jewish Hospital trying to explain her symptoms to the nurse when she interrupted me.

"Uh, Rob . . ."

"Sweetie, I'm trying to have your doctor paged to find out what your pain means."

"You need to get me to the hospital, *now*. My water just broke."

I grabbed Sammy's hand and put the other one on the small of her back. We moved as quickly as possible considering her condition. She threw an old bath towel on the back seat of the car as I put the key in the ignition. I then did the same thing I always did before hitting the gas. I started adjusting the radio station.

"Rob, this is one moment that doesn't need a soundtrack. Just drive the *fucking* car."

Even though my initial reaction was to say, "whatever you want, Ms. Daisy," I wisely stopped myself. I drove as fast as I could without risking being pulled over. My wife quickly pointed out that there was no need for such restraint.

"Sweetie, I love you more than anything. That's why we're in this situation right now. No cop is going to stop you at 12:30 on a Friday, however. For once, you've got the perfect excuse for defying authority."

For the remainder of the trip, I did my best to take her mind off her pain. I knew better than to point out the weird smell overtaking both of us, although I don't remember that being mentioned in any depiction of a woman going into labor.

"You know, Sammy, I finally found someone so perfect for me that even I couldn't fuck it up."

"Rob, that is *so* sweet. But right now the only thing I want to feel is the epidural going into my spine."

When we finally got the hospital, however, it wasn't as easy as she hoped to get situated and sedated. The nurses had a long list of questions for Sammy.

"On a scale of one to ten, how would you grade your pain?"

I didn't know how they expected anyone to answer questions objectively in this scenario. If it were me, I'd say whatever would get me the drugs fastest. After scribbling all of Sam's responses on her clipboard, the nurse told us the anesthesia would be forthcoming. I had already called Sam's parents, who were on their way up from Florida. Mine would be leaving Connecticut in a few hours. I looked at my watch and saw that we'd been up all night without even realizing it.

I didn't even feel myself falling asleep, so the next sound I heard was the nurse talking to me. "Sir! The doctor is here!"

I sprang up out of the chair next to Sammy's bed as the doctor began asking her some questions about her contractions. Then he looked at the birth canal. The doctor guided her through the pushing that I recognized from every movie or TV show I'd ever seen on childbirth. However, I didn't expect the next part.

"Look, it's nothing to be worried about, but if things don't improve when I come back then we will have to schedule an emergency caesarian."

Sure enough, they soon said they would be performing "the procedure" that afternoon. I knew there was nothing to worry about, since both Sam and the doctors kept saying so. I still decided to call Money while Sam slept. I figured this was one of those times to keep my anxiety away from her.

"Dude, it's fine. It's only fitting that you guys would have a kid that would have to come through the side door."

"Thanks for always having my back," I said.

"I've got both your backs," he assured me. "Just try to chill out until it's time."

We both tried to sleep until the procedure, although I'm sure Sammy got as little sleep as I did. This undoubtedly made me extra agitated when the male nurse asked us in a way-too-peppy tone if we were ready.

"So now let's see if we can't deliver a baby."

As he wheeled Sam towards the delivery room, he started whistling. This would have been merely annoying if it had been an actual tune, but he was clearly improvising. I was about to say something when I heard Sam giggling.

"You don't like jamming so much now, huh?"

When we got to the emergency room, the nurses assembled a partition so that I wouldn't be able to see Sammy being operated on. This was for my own good, they said.

Before I knew it, the nurse was asking us if we'd like to meet our daughter. Both of our faces instantly transformed into huge smiles as the nurse airlifted Sarah over the divider. As I held her in my arms, I felt like no one had ever produced such a perfect little person before. Although I am sure most, if not all, parents feel that way, I looked at Sammy and knew she felt the same thing.

As I handed Sarah to her, the nurse told us that they would need to run some routine tests. Sam's temperature was a little high and if Sarah's was as well, she'd need to spend the night in the NICU. Before I could even go down the dad rabbit hole of worry for the first time, my wife quickly extinguished those fears.

"Rob, don't freak. I've read about this and it happens to lots of kids. She'll be fine."

"Mr. Gross, the worst that will happen is that you will have to bring her home Monday. I'm going to let mommy get some sleep and bring this little lady to the NICU. When she's all settled in you can swing by."

I gave Sam a kiss on the forehead as she began to shut her eyes. I looked at my watch. It was late Saturday afternoon even though it felt like days since we'd gone for that Mexican dinner. While I waited for the nurse to get my daughter situated, I listened to my phone messages. I then sent out a text with the news that

Sarah was here and healthy. I also spoke to my parents who told me they'd take me for an early dinner after I went to the NICU.

"You must be so exhausted," my mom said.

I hadn't had time to feel tired, although I was sure I'd crash later. Right now, I wanted to get started being a dad and take a digital photo I could share with everyone on the text chain.

When I arrived, the nurse buzzed me through. The first thing I noticed was how much bigger Sarah was than all of the other babies. Some had a bunch of tubes hooked up to them or were enclosed in clear plastic, like when E.T. got sick. The nurse must have noticed my concern.

"Many of those babies were born prematurely. You and your wife don't have to worry about that, fortunately. "Sarah was sleeping under her little white hat when I first saw her. She had an IV and a finger clip taped to her left hand, two other sensors taped to her belly, and a clip where the umbilical cord had been. She was extremely pink with a few reddish blotches. Both of her eyelids had so much ointment slathered on them that they were almost reflective.

I had never seen anything as beautiful in my life.

"You can hold her. She won't break," the nurse joked.

I dug my fingers into the blanket that swaddled Sarah and lifted her up.

"She's got quite a set of lungs," she added.

"What do you mean?"

"When she's been up she's been crying *reallllly* loudly."

"Oh," I mumbled. "I'm sorry."

"No, it's a good thing. Crying is how babies communicate everything. You want them to be vocal at this age. It means she's healthy. It's good for the other babies to hear her so they can learn."

"I'm glad she's already showing some leadership skills or at least being commended for disrupting the group," I joked.

"I'll give you two some privacy." With that, the nurse moved on to another crib. I took a long look into those two greasy pools that covered her eyes. I watched as her chest rose and fall after each breath. She was so little that I couldn't believe those lungs were actually producing air. I stuck my finger into her little palm and she grasped it. She was still asleep, but it felt like the tightest embrace I had ever felt. I couldn't imagine ever feeling this happy. I reached into the pocket of my cargo pants and found my camera. I snapped a picture that I would print out later to put on our bedroom door for when Sam and Sarah came home.

I kissed my daughter on the forehead just as I had done to Sam.

"See you tomorrow," I whispered.

I met both proud sets of grandparents at a Greek diner right on the Queens border. It was one of those places with the countless bottles of Ouzo over the cash register. The owner's daughters seat you, wait on you, and take your check after asking if you enjoyed your meal.

When we sat down, my mom told the waitress that I had just become a father. She congratulated me and assured me that some complimentary drinks would be on their way.

My dad put his arm around me as we waited.

"Rob, I knew when you married Samantha that you had finally grown up. This is just great. Sarah is just adorable and you guys have both done a fantastic job. We wish all three of you the best of everything."

It wasn't like Sam had suddenly made me a grown up, though she definitely brought out the best in me. We brought out the best in each other. That was the point of a good relationship. Of course, now that I finally understood that, I'd be adding becoming a father to the mix. Just when you get shit figured out, everything changes and you have to start over. All this deep thought was reminding me I'd been up for almost 24 hours. I needed to finish my burger and get some sleep before coming back to the hospital in the morning.

I said my goodbyes and drove back from the diner. Sam and

I were now living in a "luxury apartment" month to month until the town house we'd bought was finished. I went into the refrigerator for a cold Rolling Rock and turned on the CD player that came with the apartment. It had five discs in there, so I just pushed shuffle. I usually liked to know exactly what song was coming up, but decided to spin the wheel. Plus, all five CDs were Dead shows from different eras.

I heard the opening strains of "Comes A Time," and immediately recognized that it was the band's final show from the University of Rochester in 1971. I took a long sip of my beer and sat on the couch as Jerry sang about somehow making it on the dreams you still believe in.

You said it, Jer. As I finally had a chance to exhale, it occurred to me that I'd be at the hospital all day tomorrow. The Chargers were at Kansas City. I knew I wouldn't be able to watch the game, nor should I even try. Maybe it was time to finally take a Sunday off, especially given the circumstances.

I'd check for updates on satellite radio. That seemed like progress.

ACKNOWLEDGMENTS

THE STORY YOU HAVE JUST READ is a work of fiction, but based on many true events. More importantly, the *spirit* of the tale is true. The advantage of "autofiction" is that things *do* seldom turn out as they do in the song (show or movie as well). I'd like to once again thank my beautiful wife, Sam, and our two kids, Sarah and Aaron. I couldn't have done it without the support of all my friends, both Delts and those without affiliation.

I would also like to acknowledge all those who gave me the confidence to keep going with this project at the very moment when I most needed it. This, of course, begins with my parents, Donald and Linda. I miss you both so much but hope you're smiling somewhere. Thanks to my sister for tolerating my abuse as kids and my Uncle Jeffrey and Aunt Eileen for their support all these years. Also, shout outs go to Daniel Chang, Sharon Lawrence, Eric Stangel, Neal Pollack, Alan Paul, Rich Blake and Murray Weiss at Catalyst Literary Management.

Lastly, I'd like to raise a glass to all the players, musicians, actors, and writers that have made things that much more enjoyable along the way.

—RLW

ABOUT THE AUTHOR

ROSS WARNER lives on Long Island with his extremely patient wife, Samantha, and their two amazing kids, Sarah and Aaron. He maintains his audio archive of every Grateful Dead concert ever played even though his two kids make it unlikely that he'll have time to listen any time soon. Ross has been writing about the three pillars of popular culture (television, music and film) since high school; his work has appeared in such magazines as *American Heritage, Cinema Retro, Hittin' The Note, Heeb,* and *Glide.* As a writer, he is probably best known for his long-running blog on the San Diego, now Los Angeles, Chargers, which landed him in the Pro Football Hall of Fame in 2002. His football writing has also been featured in *Sports Illustrated's* "SI Online" and *Blitz* Magazine, he was the featured columnist on the Chargers for *Bleacher Report* and he currently contributes pieces on pop culture to *Book & Film Globe.* His work on his other major life's obsession, the Grateful Dead, has been similarly featured in both books and magazines. He is proud to say he attended 138 Dead shows while Jerry was alive and that he is still bummed out that the Chargers bolted from San Diego to LA even though he's never lived a day in his life in San Diego. *Drunk on Sunday* is Ross's first book.

*My sister and I in the late '70s. I was clearly
already affected by my chosen football team.*

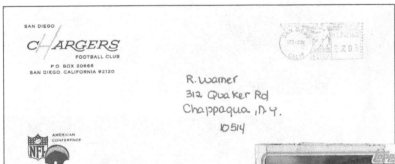

*The first response I got
from my many letters to
the Chargers. This one
returned my Dan Fouts card,
autographed.*

Jerry Garcia as I first saw him on stage, 9/18/87 at Madison Square Garden. The show was so good that I went back 137 times. [Photograph copyright © Bob Minkin]

My parents enjoying one of their many trips to Martha's Vineyard. I love and miss you guys so much.

Almost twenty-five years after writing him a fan letter, I finally got to meet Dan Fouts in 2013 when he was broadcasting a Chargers game in Washington. No, it's not the same shirt I had as a kid. Before taking this picture, Sam told him he was the reason she lost her Sundays.

After a Gov't Mule show in Atlantic City, December 2017. Taking a moment to realize how lucky I am and not just because I just saw an awesome concert. Thanks to DJ for taking the picture.

Sammy and I on our fifteenth wedding anniversary, 2018. The best decision I ever made was walking up to her at that bar.

Sammy, Sarah, and Aaron—my amazing family. I promised Aaron he could be in the next book, even though I'm scared about him reading this one.

CPSIA information can be obtained
at www.ICGtesting.com
Printed in the USA
FSHW010954261020
75234FS